Cam has been through hell and back. He was kidnapped and torn apart by scientists while the human government turned a blind eye, and he doesn't think he will ever recover. How could he? Even now that he's free, his pain and fear keep him captive.

Rocco never thought his mate would be one of his patients, but since Cam is related to one of the assassins' mates, he's Cam's doctor first and his mate second, at least for now. He wants Cam to start living again, but he understands how hard it is, since he'd been through something similar.

Cam carries his fear, while Rocco carries guilt. Neither of them is sure they'll be able to shed it and make space for love in their life. But when the warehouse where the assassins live is attacked, they'll have to face their worst fear — and hopefully, win the fight.

Rocco
Copyright © 2020 Catherine Lievens
ISBN: 978-1-4874-2975-1
Cover art by Angela Waters

Published by eXtasy Books Inc or
Devine Destinies, an imprint of eXtasy Books Inc

Look for us online at:
www.eXtasybooks.com or www.devinedestinies.com

Rocco
Council Assassins Book 10

By

Catherine Lievens

CHAPTER ONE

Rocco sucked in a breath, then pushed the door open. He pushed too hard, and it slammed against the wall, getting everyone's attention. They all turned to look at him as he stepped into the kitchen, and he looked away, using the excuse of closing the door to make sure they didn't see how embarrassed he was.

He shouldn't be. He'd been living and working with these people for years. He should consider them his family, and he did. That didn't make it easier to spend time with them, though, not with his past.

He cleared his throat and strode to the counter, where the food was piled up. Graham was the cook, and he was an excellent one. He always made sure there were enough leftovers for everyone, which helped, considering they didn't work a nine to five job. He was grateful. He was pretty sure that if he'd had to cook for himself, he would have died of hunger by now — or of food poisoning.

"Rocco," Tali said. He worked with Rocco in the infirmary, so Rocco was closer to him and his twin brother than to most people here, even though he'd taken care of every single assassin, some of them several times.

Not wanting Tali to worry, he forced himself to smile. "Having dinner?" he asked, already feeling like an idiot, because it was evident that Tali was here for that.

Tali nodded. "What about you? Are you eating with us?"

Rocco never ate with the others. There was a good reason for that, but he knew Tali wouldn't understand. None of them

1

would. Most of them didn't know what had happened, and Rocco wanted to keep things that way.

He forced himself to smile. "I'm going to put a tray together so I can take it to Cam."

"I can do that. You should sit down and eat. You've been spending a lot of time with him in the infirmary, and I'm sure you're ready to talk to other people."

Rocco took a step back. He knew Tali was saying that to be friendly and because he cared for him. He didn't understand. Rocco didn't *want* him to understand. "I'll do it. Don't worry about it. Have fun with the others."

Tali frowned. "But I can do it. It's not a problem. I work for you, after all."

Rocco shook his head. "I'm fine."

He should probably tell everyone else that he and Cam were mates, but for now, he didn't want to. He didn't know how Cam would feel about it. Cam was still in so much pain, and he had nightly nightmares. He'd been through hell and back, and Rocco wanted to shield him, to make sure he was comfortable. That came before telling everyone else they were mates.

Telling the others probably wouldn't change a lot, except for the fact that they wouldn't look at him like he was Rocco's professional responsibility. And he was. Rocco was a doctor, and Cam was in bad shape. But there was a lot more to it, and everyone would realize that as soon as they found out. Maybe then they wouldn't ask to take the tray to Cam in place of Rocco. It didn't matter, though. As long as Cam was uncomfortable telling everyone, he wouldn't.

Besides, Cam wasn't the only reason Rocco was avoiding the assassins and their mates. He always had, and he would continue to do it. It was already nerve-racking enough to deal with Cam and making sure he didn't get hurt. Rocco needed to be a hundred percent sure he wouldn't hurt the people he lived with, either.

Some days, it sounded ridiculous even to himself, but after what had happened, after what he'd done, he couldn't take chances. He couldn't allow himself to because he didn't know what he would do if something happened and someone got hurt. Probably leave the warehouse and the assassins behind. But even though he did his best to keep them at a distance, they were his only family. He didn't want to lose them. He just wanted them to stay at a comfortable distance, at least for him.

Ignoring everyone who was sitting around the table talking, Rocco put together a tray. Cam needed to eat so he would heal faster and stay healthy, but since Rocco knew that he didn't enjoy eating right now, he tried to put together food that would be appealing.

"That's for Cam?" Ox asked.

Rocco jerked, almost dropping the fork he'd been putting onto the tray. "I didn't hear you," he said when Ox arched a brow at him.

"I can see that. So? Is the tray for Cam?"

Rocco nodded. "He needs to eat."

"Of course he does. You're taking good care of him, aren't you?"

Rocco glared at Ox. "What do you think?"

Ox shook his head. "I was just asking. I know you wouldn't hurt him."

Maybe he wasn't quite right about that, but Rocco didn't say it. "I'm doing my best. He has a long way to go, though."

Ox's smile faded. "I know. I'm terrified that he won't be able to."

Normally, Rocco wouldn't take the time to reassure Ox. He would move away from him as soon as possible, just in case. But Ox was Cam's brother, and that meant they were family. Rocco wasn't sure how to feel about that yet, but he supposed he would get used to it.

"I think he'll be fine. I don't know how long it will take him to heal, and I can't promise you he'll be like he was before, but he has a lot to live for. He has you and your mate. He's free."

Ox cocked his head as if he didn't understand what Rocco was saying. "He also has *you*."

Rocco shrugged. "I'm his doctor, sure."

"You're more than that."

Rocco was. No matter how much he tried to ignore it—and he wasn't trying very hard—he was Cam's mate. He didn't know what Cam wanted yet, though, and he wasn't about to ask him. Cam was in pain, and he was struggling. This was one more thing that Rocco would dump on his shoulders, and he couldn't deal with that, not for a while.

That was fine with Rocco. He didn't mind keeping it a secret, even though it made things awkward sometimes. People didn't understand why he was so fixated on Cam. They thought he was worried about his health, and he was. That wasn't his main reason to hover, though. He was fixated on Cam because he wanted him.

Rocco shook himself. He shouldn't be thinking about one of his patients that way, even though the patient was his mate. It wasn't ethical. Of course, there were a lot of things that weren't ethical at play here. Rocco and Cam were mates, and that trumped everything, including the doctor-patient bond. There was also the fact that there were no other doctors in the warehouse. Rocco was it for everyone, and that included Cam. The twins could take care of him for most things, but if something else happened, it would be down to Rocco. There was no way around that. Win wasn't about to get another doctor, not when the assassins were a secret group within the council.

Of course some people, like Julian, found out about them.

He was now living with them, even though it was weird because he wasn't an assassin and he didn't have any special power the way they did. He also hadn't gone through what they'd all gone through, including Rocco. He hadn't been tortured. He hadn't been changed.

And it was a good thing. Rocco knew that Julian didn't like the fact that he was just a normal shifter, but that was the last thing that mattered.

What *did* matter was that Rocco needed to get to Cam. He grabbed the tray and forced himself to smile at Ox. "Don't worry. I'm taking care of him. I'll make sure he eats."

"I know you will. I'm still worried, though. But I'm glad he has you."

He probably wouldn't if he knew what was in Rocco's past, but Rocco couldn't talk about that. He couldn't say anything about it, not to Ox, and not to anyone. Instead, he nodded curtly. "I don't know what the future holds for us, but I'll make sure he'll be okay." Even if it was the last thing Rocco did—even if it meant leaving Cam's life and never coming back.

Cam hated the infirmary. He knew he needed to be here. He was wounded. He was in pain. It would take him a while to recover from what had been done to him.

He still hated it, though.

It didn't matter how much he needed to be here. He wanted to leave. The sight of the infirmary, the smells lingering around him and on his skin—all of that brought him back to the lab. It had looked like this room did, and Cam had to work hard not to panic every five minutes.

He knew he wasn't in the lab anymore. He knew no one here would hurt him. He had his brother back, and he'd met his mate. They would make sure nothing happened to him.

Knowing that didn't help as much as it should.

It was mostly the smells. Every time Cam closed his eyes, he felt panic closing in on him. When he opened them, it was slightly easier to deal with. He was still in the infirmary, with hospital beds and medical supplies, but this place was more cheerful. It wasn't as dark as the lab had been. It had windows, and the sun streamed through them during the day. It was an infirmary, and it was sterile looking, but it also looked like a home.

It was Cam's home, and it would be for a while.

The smells were hard to deal with, though. Even now that he'd opened his eyes, he couldn't get the smells out of his nose. It was a mix of disinfectant and coldness, of blood and his body healing. It made his chest tighten, and he knew he was going to have a panic attack if he didn't do something.

But what? He'd never had panic attacks before. He had no idea how to deal with them. He knew what Rocco had told him about them, but it didn't help as much as Cam had hoped it would.

He needed to do something. He needed to get out of here. *Now.*

He struggled to sit up, his entire chest feeling like it was on fire. He knew what had been done to him, even though he'd lost consciousness almost from the beginning. His chest had been opened so that the scientists working on him could look at him, at his insides, while he shifted. That meant that his entire torso was one huge scar, and it still hurt. He suspected it would for a while.

He managed to push through the pain, though. He knew staying in bed would make things worse. He swung his legs to the side, and he was already breathless. He panted through it, pressing one foot on the floor. It was cool against his skin, and it helped a bit, but not enough. He needed more. He needed to get out.

He put his other foot down, made sure he was as steady as

he could be, took a deep breath, and pushed.

He was on his feet for a glorious five seconds before he lost his balance. He'd suspected that would happen, and he hated it. He hated feeling vulnerable the way he did. He hated needing people to do even the simplest things and being stuck in bed, unable to do anything.

Unable to escape the nightmares.

He hit the floor hard. The pain and shock pushed the air out of his lungs, and he struggled to suck in a breath. He knew he had to, because if he didn't, it would make the panic attack even worse. He supposed he should be grateful the pain was distracting him from it. He was still freaking out, but it was easier not to focus on that but instead on the pain that had seized his chest and most of his body.

Cam twisted onto his side and curled himself into a tight ball. He knew that wouldn't help, but he couldn't help it. It was pure instinct for him to curl up against the pain. He managed to breathe once, then twice, before he heard the door open.

Great. Now Rocco was going to freak out. Or maybe it was Ox. Whoever it was, their reaction would be the same as Rocco's anyway.

"Cam?" Rocco's voice held a hint of panic as he realized that Cam wasn't in his bed.

Cam groaned. He couldn't do anything else.

"Fuck," Rocco muttered. Cam heard a clang, then Rocco's footsteps coming closer. He closed his eyes. He didn't want his mate to see him like this. He didn't want *anyone* to see him like this. There was no other way, though. He knew he wouldn't be able to get himself back into bed on his own.

"Oh, sweetheart. What did you do?" Rocco asked as he crouched next to Cam.

Cam forced himself to open his eyes. The first thing he saw was Rocco reaching for him, and Cam jerked back. That, too, was instinct. He knew Rocco wouldn't hurt him. He was his doctor, and more importantly, he was his mate. Cam couldn't help it, though.

He tried to ignore the pain in Rocco's eyes and forced himself to think through the panic. He breathed in and out, and now that the pain was receding, it was easier. When he felt better, he looked at Rocco. "I'm sorry. I didn't mean to jerk back the way I did."

Rocco shook his head. "It's fine."

It wasn't, but Cam couldn't help it. He might know Rocco wouldn't hurt him, but it didn't mean he trusted him not to. The fact that they were in the infirmary didn't help, either.

Cam put his hands on the floor and tried to get at least into a sitting position, but it was hard. He felt like he'd run a marathon, or like he climbed Mount Everest. Still, with only a little help from Rocco, he managed to sit up. He was breathless, but he wasn't finished. He wanted to do this on his own, and he got his feet under himself, then used the bed to pull himself up.

That didn't last long. His legs couldn't hold his weight, and he knew he wouldn't be able to get back into bed on his own. He needed to accept Rocco's help, no matter how little he wanted to.

He swallowed. His eyes burned with tears he didn't want to shed. He knew Rocco wouldn't care. He wanted to help, and Cam wished he could accept that help. He didn't want to look weak, though. That was when people hurt you the most. Still, he had to. He looked at Rocco. "I don't think I can do this on my own," he quietly admitted.

At least Rocco didn't look at him with pity in his eyes. He didn't try to patronize him. He didn't say anything at all, actually. Instead, he gently wrapped Cam into his arms and hauled him up.

That hurt, too, but for whatever reason, it also helped. Cam found himself leaning against Rocco's chest, smelling him. He realized it was the bond. His otter wanted to be close to their mate, and he wished he could give it that. He wished he trusted Rocco. He wanted to.

But Rocco was a doctor. He was Cam's mate, but he was also someone Cam barely knew. It would take time for them to get used to being in each other's life. Cam supposed it was a good thing that he wasn't going anywhere anytime soon.

"Are you okay?" Rocco asked.

Cam didn't know how to answer that. He didn't know if he was okay, or if he ever would be. He didn't know if he would ever be able to trust Rocco and to let him in. He hated the pain he'd caused his mate, but he had no clue how not to, how not to react instinctively when people tried to touch him.

Maybe he was broken. Maybe he would never recover.

Rocco realized he needed to stop panicking. He wouldn't have panicked if the person on the floor had been anyone other than his mate, but it *was* Cam, and it was hard to think through the fear.

Rocco knew what Cam had been trying to do, of course. He'd been vocal about the fact that he hated being stuck in bed. Rocco suspected there was more to it, but he hadn't pushed. Maybe it was time to do that, though. It was obvious something was wrong with Cam—something more than his body still healing and the mental scars—and Rocco wouldn't be able to help him until he knew. Of course, Cam would have to be willing to tell him, and he wasn't sure that would happen.

He hadn't missed the way Cam had shied away from him earlier. He didn't blame him. Even though they were mates, Cam had been through so much. What was worse was that he'd been hurt by a doctor, by someone who should have helped him. And that was what Rocco was. He was a doctor, and he was taking care of Cam. It would be easy for him to hurt Cam, and Cam knew that.

Rocco tried to be as gentle as possible as he put Cam down onto the bed. He couldn't ignore the grimace of pain on Cam's face, and he hated it. He hated everything that had to do with it. He wanted to do so much more for his mate, but he didn't think there *was* more he could do, not with things the way they were. Maybe if Cam let him in, but Rocco didn't think Cam was ready for that. He didn't know if Cam would ever be ready.

"Where are you hurting?" he asked as soon as Cam was back on the bed.

Cam shook his head. "I'm fine."

"I need to be sure. Please. You could have reopened one of the wounds in the fall."

Cam scowled, but he finally allowed Rocco to touch him. Rocco was so used to doing this by now that it took him only a handful of minutes to make sure Cam really was okay. He was no doubt in pain, but his wounds were still the way they'd been a few hours earlier when Rocco had last checked them. There was no blood, nothing that would show Rocco that Cam had injured himself when he'd fallen.

Rocco breathed more easily. His movements slowed down, and Cam took the occasion to try to push him away again. He was weak, though. He hadn't hurt himself, but he was nowhere near peak health. Everything was exhausting, but especially trying to get out of bed and hurting himself in the process because he'd fallen. His movements were weak when he tried to push away Rocco's hand, but Rocco allowed him to do so anyway.

"You're fine," he said. Cam snorted, and Rocco knew why. "What I meant is that you're as fine as you were a few hours ago. I know you're not okay, though."

Cam shook his head. "I don't think I'll ever be okay."

Rocco bit his lower lip. He wanted to ask questions, but he wasn't sure Cam would answer them. Still, he wouldn't know until he did. "Can you tell me what happened?"

Cam pressed his lips together and shook his head. "Nothing."

Rocco sighed. He knew that would happen. He knew what Cam had been trying to do. He hated being in the infirmary, but so far, there was no other way to do this. Cam needed to be here because of his health issues. Rocco would allow him to move out as soon as he could, but in the meantime, Cam would have to deal with this, no matter how much he hated it.

"You know you can tell me anything," Rocco said. He already knew how Cam would react to that, too.

Cam looked away. He'd been isolating himself even from Rocco and his brother. He didn't want to talk. He didn't want to spend time with people. After the first few days, he'd started closing off, and Rocco didn't know what to do or how to help. He wanted to, but the only thing he could do was to continue taking care of Cam, so he went back to the door and picked up the tray he'd put together. He'd left it there when he'd seen that Cam wasn't on the bed, and he hoped the food wasn't too cold. "I went downstairs to get you dinner," he said.

Cam barely looked at him. "I'm not hungry."

Rocco wasn't surprised about that, either. Cam only ate when he had to, and Rocco didn't want to force him. He put the tray down on the table next to Cam's bed, then twisted the table until Cam could get the plate if he wanted to. He took his own plate and sat in one of the chairs next to the bed and started eating.

It was the only way Cam ate. Rocco didn't know what had happened to him in the lab. He'd found some files, but they were precise only when it came to the medical procedures he'd been subjected to. Not all the scientists had taken notes. Some of them had probably wanted to keep what they were doing a secret, and Rocco resented that. It meant that he didn't know how to help and that he *couldn't* help as much as he should. It was entirely possible that the scientists had put poison or sedatives into Cam's food. That would explain why he was always more eager to eat fruit that he could peel himself or that he could see was in one piece than anything that had been cooked or served on an open plate. He was wary, even though so far, nothing had happened to him in the warehouse.

Rocco realized it would take him time to get used to this, and even more time to get over what had been done to him, if he ever did. The thought that he wouldn't was terrifying. Rocco wanted Cam to be okay. He wanted Cam to be able to enjoy life, to live it to the fullest. It would take a while for his body to heal, even with the Nix taking turns healing the wounds, but Rocco knew that eventually, Cam would be okay physically.

His mental health was another issue, though. Rocco had no idea how to deal with that. He was a doctor, but he took care of the body, not the mind. It was obvious to him and to anyone else who regularly met with Cam that he needed more help, but Rocco didn't know how to give it to him. He wanted to. That wasn't the problem. The problem was that he didn't know if Cam would accept that kind of help, and he didn't want to overstep.

Rocco smiled when Cam finally reached for his plate. He'd made sure to grab a small piece of dessert, too. It was pie, and he knew Cam had a sweet tooth, no matter how wary he was. He wanted Cam to be happy, and so far, this was the only way he'd found to make that happen. Eating sweets made him smile, and Rocco wanted that to continue. He wanted things to get better, both for himself and for Cam. He'd been over the moon when he'd realized Cam was his mate, then incredibly hurt because of what Cam had been through. Now, though, he also had to face the fact that he and Cam might never be together.

It hurt. Rocco realized it was a selfish emotion, and he didn't like that he felt that way. He couldn't help it, though. He wanted to do more. He wanted him and Cam to be together like mates. But even if Cam healed, there was no way to know if he would look at Rocco that way. There was no way to know if he would ever be able to separate Rocco from all the pain he was feeling right now. Rocco could only hope and wait, no matter how frustrating it was. But whatever Cam decided, Rocco would make sure he had what he needed and wanted. There was no other way out of it. *Rocco* wouldn't have it any other way.

Cam wanted to trust Rocco. He really did. Rocco was taking care of him beyond what a normal doctor would. He brought Cam breakfast, lunch, and dinner even when Cam told him he wasn't hungry. He also always sat with Cam to eat with him. Cam was grateful. He didn't like being alone, probably because he'd spent too much time on his own when he'd been in the lab. On the other hand, though, he also often felt the need to push everyone away, including Rocco and Ox.

Cam was a mess. He knew that, and he wanted it to stop. He didn't know how to make that happen, though.

He quietly ate his dinner while sneaking glances at Rocco, who wasn't even looking at him. They were mates, and Rocco had been doing his best to help. He'd been there for Cam through it all—the pain, the hatred, the nightmares. He wasn't going anywhere. He would be there until Cam told him he didn't want him to be. Cam's otter was on board with trusting Rocco, and possibly, bonding with him. That was all it wanted, and some days, Cam wanted to give in.

But he couldn't. His human side didn't trust Rocco, no matter how much his heart told him he needed to. Part of him knew that Rocco wouldn't hurt him. The other part was terrified that he would end up in the lab once again. He felt broken most of the time, and he didn't know how to fix himself. He didn't even know if he could.

Cam didn't like silence. Rocco never pushed him to talk, but usually, he was the one who chatted a lot when they ate. He told Cam small anecdotes about the warehouse and the people who lived in it. It was still hard for Cam to believe that there was a group of professional killers and that his brother's mate was one of them. Ox had explained his mate didn't actually kill people, but rather, he shimmered the assassins around, but still. He was one of them, and it was strange to think that way. It was also strange to think that Ox's mate was part of this kind of thing. So far, Cam had met a few assassins when they'd needed medical attention, but he barely wanted to talk to his brother and his mate, and he wasn't eager to talk to them, either.

Cam didn't hate it, though. He knew it was thanks to the assassins that he'd been freed from the lab, and that they'd made sure the scientists who'd been hurting him would never hurt anyone else. It gave Cam a fierce satisfaction, and he didn't care one bit if the scientists had been killed. It was what they deserved. They'd hurt him and countless other people, and they would no doubt have continued if they were alive. This way, Cam could be sure he'd been the last victim.

But the silence that lingered in the room reminded him too much of the lab. There had been silence there too, only interrupted by his screams of pain. It was so easy to think about that time when nothing was said, and he wanted to break the silence, but he didn't know how. He didn't know what to tell

Rocco. He had nothing to talk about. His entire life right now was in the infirmary, in his bed, and nothing exciting happened. Rocco was often there with him, but he did leave, so he would have more things to say.

"This is good," Cam murmured. He needed to break the silence, and he hoped Rocco would take the hint.

Luckily for him, Rocco did. He finally looked up from his plate and smiled at Cam. "It is. Graham is a great cook. I'm glad Win hired him."

Cam frowned. He was starting to recognize the names, but he still didn't know who was a professional killer and who wasn't. The cook probably wasn't, but he wanted to be sure. "He's a mate, right?" he asked.

Rocco nodded. "He is. That's not how he came to us, though."

"Can you tell me about it?"

"It's not a secret, so yes, I can tell you about it. It all started with Milo. Well, I guess it started with Noel, actually. Milo was his personal assistant, and when Noel left the firm he worked for, Milo stayed behind. He hated his new boss, though, and as soon as he could, he came to work with Noel. Graham is his best friend, and a professional cook. That's why he came to work here. Milo already knew him and could vouch for him. Then he and Win realized they were mates, and here we are."

It all sounded so incredible to Cam. Even before he'd been taken, his life had been boring. He'd been a normal guy with a normal family. Well, as normal as a family could be. But there hadn't been anything extraordinary in his life, and now, everything had changed. Now he was part of the life of the assassins who lived in the warehouse. He was here, and through Rocco's words, he was starting to get to know all of them. He wanted more, but he knew he wasn't ready for it. Eventually, he hoped he would consider the assassins his family. He didn't care what they did for a living. They'd saved him.

In the beginning, he'd been hesitant, and he'd had a long chat with his brother. Ox knew a lot more than Cam did about the people who lived in the warehouse, and he'd explained that while yes, they were professional killers, they didn't kill just anyone. They only accepted the jobs they could deal with, and all of those came from the council, which meant that the people the assassins were contracted to kill deserved it. They were drug dealers, shifter traffickers, and they hurt people.

So no, Cam didn't have a problem with what everyone in the house did. He also couldn't imagine himself leaving the warehouse and going to live on his own. Even if he thought about the future in one or two years, it was impossible for him to think that he would be on his own. He never wanted to be on his own again. He'd spent so much time alone in the lab that the thought made him uncomfortable.

"I guess it's been a chain reaction," Rocco continued. It took a second for Cam to realize what he was talking about. "It's like every mate brings someone with them, and that someone finds their mate with us."

Cam nodded. "Like Ox. He and Dasha realized they were mates, and then he brought me in, and I met you."

Rocco smiled at Cam. "Exactly. It's weird, but it's also a good thing. All of us have been through so much. We're also used to being alone. Things are changing, and I think it's for the better, even though I'm not sure our family can stay the way it was before. We're not just professional killers anymore. We're building families, and that means something is going to have to change."

"You think the council will try to stop it?"

"I doubt it. I know it might feel like they're the bad guys here, since they created our little group, but they're not. Most of the council members want us to be happy, just like every other shifter. They use us for our abilities, but they would never force us into anything. I have no doubt that if someone wants to leave, they will be allowed to. Of course, there will be restraints like not talking about what they used to do, but then, isn't that the case with every job?"

Cam didn't know. Most days, he had a hard time remembering his life before the lab. If he tried to think about his past, the only thing that came to mind was pain and fear. There was more to it, of course, but it felt like a different life, like someone else had lived it.

He couldn't believe Rocco would want to be with him when he was in this state. Who would? They were mates, but Cam truly was broken, and he didn't know if he could be fixed. It had to be the bond. That was why Cam was attracted to Rocco and wanted him in his life, and no doubt, the same went for Rocco. Of course he wanted to spend time with Cam. He could feel the pull. But what if he stopped feeling it? Would he eventually be able to forget Cam?

Cam wasn't sure of anything right now, and most days, he felt like he would never be sure of anything else again. He knew it wasn't true, but he wished he was already done with this part of his life. He had no idea what the future with Rocco would be like. He had no idea if he and Rocco would *have* a future together considering everything. But he had hope, at least most of the time.

The other times, well, the only thing he could see when he thought of the future was darkness, and he hated it.

CHAPTER TWO

Being the doctor for the council assassins was a strange job. Some days, Rocco and the twins were crazy busy. When one of the assassins was wounded, they needed to focus on him or her, and that usually meant long hours. Most of the time, though, their job consisted of hanging around waiting and cleaning the infirmary. On the one hand, it was a good thing, since it meant that the assassins were good at their jobs and healthy, but on the other, it was kind of boring. Of course, things were different now that Cam was in the infirmary. Still, having a doctor and two Nix taking care of him was a bit too much. There was nothing they could do twenty-four-seven, which was why Rocco was usually the one who stuck with Cam.

But the twins needed something to do, which was why they were cleaning the infirmary right now. They were used to it, and Rocco couldn't help but smile at the banter between them. He'd worked with them for a few years, even though he'd been the assassins' doctor for longer than that, and he was grateful for their presence. Things had been hard when he'd been working alone. Rocco hadn't had access to a Nix who could heal the assassins, and he'd needed to do everything on his own. It meant that whoever got wounded back then was out of commission for a while. Now, it mostly wasn't a problem. Unless someone was badly injured, they were usually back to work in a few days.

Cam was different, though. Not only wasn't he an assassin, but it would take him much longer than a week to heal. Rocco kind of wanted to wrap him in cotton and make sure that nothing else could hurt him, and he wanted to keep everyone away from him because he knew how uncomfortable Cam was with people, but he was also aware of the fact that Cam needed this. He needed people hanging around. He needed to have as normal a life as he could, considering everything. It wasn't easy after the time he'd spent in the lab, but having the twins around probably helped, even though Cam barely talked to them most days. The twins didn't mind. They might not be assassins, but they'd been through a lot too, and they understood where Cam was coming from. They'd had more time to heal, and they knew how hard his recovery would be. That was why they weren't pushing, and Rocco wasn't, either.

The infirmary door slammed open, making all of them jump. Rocco's attention went straight to Cam, who was trying to scramble up the bed to press his back against the wall. He didn't need to, but of course, he was acting on instinct.

Rocco ignored whoever had entered and went to his mate. "Relax. It's just a patient," he murmured.

Cam turned wide eyes toward him. "How do you know that?"

They both looked at the door at the same time. Rocco groaned when he saw what was waiting for him. "What happened this time?" he asked.

He gently patted Cam's thigh, then went to Julian, who was cradling his arm against his body. Roark was standing behind him, looking sheepish as he rubbed the back of his neck. "I might have gone overboard," he said.

Julian scowled at him. "Overboard? You broke my arm!"

Roark rolled his eyes. This wasn't the first time Julian ended up in the infirmary, and it was always for the same reason. He wanted to be a council assassin, but the problem was that all the assassins had something *more*. They'd been in labs, and they'd been modified. Roark had the power to enter people's minds and make them believe they were in other places. Julian, on the other hand, was just a shifter. He was good at his job, or at least that was what Rocco had been told, but he couldn't compare.

That was also why Julian had been jealous of Roark, and why he'd tried to get to him several times. Rocco still didn't know if he'd been planning to kill Roark, but knowing Julian now, he doubted it. Still, Julian was in trouble, and he was running from someone. That was why he was living with the assassins. It couldn't be easy for him, considering how free he'd been before and how stuck he was in the warehouse now, but he never complained.

Instead, he trained with the assassins, which often ended in him getting hurt.

Rocco gestured at the bed closer to the door. "Sit down."

Julian started to salute but winced in pain. "Got it, Doc," he said instead.

If it really was a broken arm, it would be easy enough to heal him. Rocco looked at the twins, but to his surprise, Tali was doing a good job ignoring him and looking away. It made Rocco frown, but he didn't have the time to check what was happening. "Jolyn? Do you want to come here and heal Julian?"

Jolyn looked at his brother, then back at Rocco, and nodded. "Sure. Give me a few seconds to wash my hands. I'll be right there."

"He's not going anywhere anyway."

Julian groaned. "How do you know that? Maybe I'm planning to run away."

Rocco rolled his eyes—again. "You want to run away with a broken arm? Be my guest. You're giving me more work than all the assassins put together these days, so I wouldn't object."

"It's not my fault Roark is a brute."

"You wanted to train," Roark cried out.

"To train, yes. Not to get my arm broken."

"*You* insisted I use my power."

"I didn't expect you to attack me while I was distracted. Why did you make me see that I was in the forest and then attack me only seconds later? You could at least have given me some time to get used to what I was seeing."

"I never gave time to my marks."

"I'm not a mark."

"Yet."

Rocco smiled. Those two were always at each other's throats, but it was evident that they were friends. It was a good thing. Julian had to feel a bit odd being in the warehouse with all of them. He wasn't a mate, but he also wasn't an assassin. He didn't belong to either group, and he'd only recently moved in.

Julian turned his attention to Rocco. "I'm sorry I'm giving you so much work."

Rocco shrugged. "It's fine. At least my life isn't boring."

Julian's eyes glittered. "Right, because you only work when someone is wounded." His gaze quickly went to Cam, but it didn't linger there. "What do you do when you're *not* working?"

Rocco blinked. "What do you mean?"

"Exactly what I said. What do you do when there's no one in the infirmary to take care of? And how did you become the doctor for the assassins? Have you always been a doctor, or is this a second job? And who have you healed more often? Please, tell me it's Roark."

Rocco shook his head and ignored the steady stream of words coming out of Julian's mouth. As soon as Jolyn got back, they went to work on Julian. Rocco also ignored the winces and groans and the way Julian kept wiggling, and he and Jolyn patched him up.

Julian never stopped talking, and Rocco wasn't surprised.

He seemed to have an endless list of topics to ask about. He had to breathe every so often, though, and Rocco took advantage of one of those moments to gently push Julian toward the door, where Roark was waiting. "You're all patched up. There's nothing else we can do."

Julian blinked and looked down at his arm. "Already?"

Rocco felt the need to roll his eyes yet again, but he was pretty sure that if he continued, they would eventually fall out of his face. "Be careful for a few days. The bone is healed, but it's still fragile and sensitive. Take it easy, make sure you don't get into another fight, and for the love of God, don't train."

This time, Julian *did* salute Rocco. "Got it, Doc. Do you need to see me again?"

"Please don't come back. You never stop talking."

Julian grinned. "It's part of my charm."

Rocco wasn't sure whether or not Julian was flirting with him, but it didn't matter. He pointed at the door. "You can go. *Now.*" Rocco would go crazy if he didn't.

Cam knew he was scowling, but he couldn't help it. He hadn't missed the way Rocco had only asked for help from one of the twins, which meant that he'd left the other one to babysit Cam.

Cam didn't need to be babysat. He wasn't a kid. He was an adult, and even though he was in bad shape, that wouldn't change.

He wouldn't deny he'd been frightened when the door had slammed open. He probably should be used to that by now, considering how many times Julian had already come in since he'd arrived, but he wasn't. Loud noises still made him jump, and his first instinct was always to run away, or in this case, press himself against the wall and pray everything would be okay.

Everything *was* okay. Logically, Cam knew that no one could come inside the warehouse. He might not have seen the security measures, but both Ox and Rocco had explained them to him. He knew he was safe here. The only people who could come to the infirmary were the ones who lived here, including Julian.

But some things, like reacting the way Cam had, were hard to leave behind. Cam might know he was okay, but it always took his brain a few seconds to go along with the program. Those few seconds were enough to make a fool of himself, and it was something he hated.

He also hated being babysat.

He turned his attention to Tali, who was hovering close by, not even faking working. He knew Tali didn't have a say in this, since Rocco was his boss, and he was trying very hard not to be rude, but it wasn't easy.

Then Tali looked up at him and smiled. "Thank you," he murmured.

Cam frowned. "What are you thanking me for?"

Tali's gaze flickered toward Julian, then went back to Cam. "I didn't want to be close to him."

Cam's frown deepened. "Why? Has he done something to you? Has he hurt you?" Cam might be wounded, but that wouldn't stop him from kicking Julian's ass if he'd hurt Tali.

Julian was new here, just like Cam. He wasn't a council assassin. He was just a guy, and Cam didn't know if he trusted him. Everyone seemed to, but Tali's words were worrying.

Tali's eyes widened, and he shook his head. "Oh, no. He hasn't hurt me in any way. He hasn't even talked to me."

"Then why don't you want to be close to him?"

Cam was pretty sure that wasn't his business, but it was a nice change. He wasn't used to talking like this with anyone but Rocco. Even when the twins were close by in the infirmary, Cam stayed isolated. It was safer. He and the twins weren't friends, but this felt good, almost like Cam had gone back in time to his old self.

Tali looked at Julian again. "He's my mate." He sighed. "And he doesn't know it. He's a shifter, so he would have to come close to me to smell it."

"I see." And Cam did. His situation with Rocco was different, since they both knew they were mates, but it was also similar. "You don't know what to do with it, do you?"

Tali's eyes widened. "How do you know?"

Cam shrugged. "Call it instinct." And being in the same situation.

Of course, it wasn't *exactly* the same. Tali wasn't wounded, and he didn't depend on Julian. He could stay away from him without too many problems, but that wasn't the case for Cam. Rocco wasn't going anywhere. He was Cam's doctor, which meant that Cam would see him every day even if he didn't want to.

But to his surprise, most days, he *did* want to. He wasn't ready for them to be together, or even for them to be friends, but having Rocco hanging around was both soothing and irritating. Cam was a mess of feelings and emotions, and he had no idea how to deal with them. He wasn't sure he could at this moment, but he supposed that once his body started healing, his mind would, too.

The door closed, and both he and Tali looked up to see Julian wasn't there anymore. Rocco was coming back toward them, his entire attention on Cam. Tali took a step back, and Cam scowled a bit at him, wanting him to come back.

He didn't mind spending time alone with Rocco. He was getting used to it. What he did mind was that Rocco always fussed over him. It wasn't just because he was his doctor, either. To whoever looked at them, it had to be obvious there was something between them. It was in the way Rocco took care of Cam, which didn't look anything like the way he took care of everyone else in the warehouse.

"How are you feeling?" Rocco asked as soon as he reached Cam's bed. "He didn't mean to scare you. He's just . . . Julian."

Cam narrowed his eyes. Once again, he didn't know how to feel about this. He was annoyed about the fact that Rocco clearly thought that he was still freaking out, wary about why Rocco would want to check in on him to make sure he was okay, but also soothed by the concern. Rocco cared for him. He knew that. *He* might even care for Rocco, although he wasn't sure how that would feel. But he knew that Rocco wanted him to be okay and that it was why he was overbearing sometimes.

Which was precisely the case right now.

Cam forced himself to look at Rocco. "I'm fine."

"Are you sure? Because he really didn't mean anything by it. He's just like that. He doesn't think before acting most of the time, which is why he always ends up wounded and in here. He's a loudmouth, but he wouldn't hurt a fly."

"I told you I'm fine," Cam snapped. He regretted his tone of voice as soon as the words were out of his mouth, but he couldn't take them back. Besides, he didn't want to take them back. He wanted Rocco to understand.

Cam might be wounded, in pain, and traumatized, but he wasn't less of a man for that. He didn't need to be coddled or babysat.

Rocco took a step back.

Cam regretted his tone even more. He hadn't meant to hurt his mate.

"I'm sorry. I was just making sure you were okay," Rocco said.

Cam did his best to soften his voice. "I am. I *told* you I am. I don't need you to fuss, and I don't need a babysitter."

Rocco frowned. "A babysitter?"

"You left Tali with me while Jolyn took care of Julian."

Rocco shook his head. "I didn't ask Tali to stay with you, though. I didn't call him to me because I didn't need him. I don't need two Nix to heal a broken arm. Jolyn did a great job, and besides, I've noticed that Tali doesn't like being around Julian."

Cam's heart softened. He should have known better. How could he, though, when he never allowed Rocco close? "I apologize," he said.

Rocco shook his head again. "You have nothing to apologize for. I'm the one who needs to continue apologizing. I never meant to be overbearing. I just care about your well-being, Cam."

Cam knew that was the truth. He knew he should be grateful, and he was. He was also a lot of other things, though, like annoyed, wary, distraught. Terrified. He hated feeling that way, but he didn't know how he could deal with it.

Rocco realized he was overbearing. He'd been working hard to give Cam space, but obviously, he hadn't been doing a good job. He needed to try harder. The last thing he wanted was for Cam to get angry with him and push him away even more than he already was. No matter how little Cam liked it, Rocco needed to be with him. He needed to keep an eye on him to make sure he healed the way he should.

"All right. Since you're okay, I'm going back to work," Rocco said.

Cam sighed. "I didn't mean to make you run," he said.

"You're not making me run. You were clear. You need space and time, and I'm trying to give that to you. Now that I know you're okay, I can."

"But Tali and Jolyn are busy," Cam whined.

Rocco did his best not to smile. He didn't want Cam to

think he was making fun of him when he wasn't. "They have things to do."

"What? I'm the only patient."

"You are, which is a good thing. We do need to keep the infirmary up to date and make sure that we have all the medicines and everything else we might need if someone comes home wounded."

"You didn't need anything when Julian came in."

"Because he had a broken arm. It's easily fixed, but it's also one of the simplest and least lethal wounds I see around here. Trust me. When one of the assassins gets hurt, it's usually pretty bad."

Cam grimaced. "I can imagine, considering their job." He exhaled. "Look, I know I just told you that I needed you to take a step back, but I'm bored. I hate being here. I want out of the infirmary."

The whine was still in Cam's words, but Rocco ignored it. "You're not in good shape," he said. He couldn't allow Cam to leave, not when Cam could be hurt again. He needed to keep him safe.

Cam scowled at him. "Don't you think I know that? You've been telling me often enough. That's not what I meant, though. I know I can't just leave this place. I can barely walk on my own. But it's not like you have me hooked up to anything here. Beds are the same everywhere, right? I could maybe find somewhere else to be, maybe even a couch. And if someone helped me, I could even use the bathroom again. I hate this thing." He gestured at his groin, and Rocco knew he was talking about the catheter.

Rocco forced himself to breathe through the panic. Cam wasn't saying he wanted to leave. He was just bored with being in the infirmary, and Rocco understood that. He would be bored, too, if he had to stare at the same four walls day in and day out.

He couldn't keep Cam locked up in the infirmary. No matter how much he hated thinking about Cam leaving him behind, it wasn't happening yet, and if it did eventually, he would have to deal with it. He couldn't forbid Cam to live, not when Cam hadn't had the possibility for years. Not when he was finally free to do it.

Rocco sucked in a breath. "I'll take you for a walk," he said.

Cam blinked. "Will you?"

Rocco nodded. "I could find you a wheelchair, but it would be hard to navigate the stairs with it. If you're okay, I'd like to carry you outside."

Cam's smile faded. "I'm not a baby. I don't need to be carried around."

"I never said anything like that. I know you don't like feeling like you need other people, especially me, but in this case, it's either that or you stay here. Like I said, there are too many stairs for a wheelchair. Unfortunately, we're not equipped for that, and the twins are busy. It's your choice. I can carry you to the roof so you can get some fresh air, or you can stay here."

The scowl on Cam's face told Rocco he didn't like it. Rocco didn't mind. He wanted to give Cam what he needed, but Cam was wounded. He was in pain most of the day because he refused the painkillers Rocco wanted to give him. Every movement would be hell for him, and while this would be easier with a wheelchair, Rocco hadn't been lying. There were too many stairs, especially since the only place they could go to was the roof.

"Fine."

Rocco cocked his head at Cam, wondering if he'd heard that right. "Fine?"

Cam narrowed his eyes at him.

Rocco was used to having Cam glare or scowl when he was displeased, so he wasn't fazed by it.

"I said fine. You can carry me to the roof."

Rocco nodded. "I will, then." He moved closer to Cam, whose eyes widened.

"You mean now?" Cam asked.

"We can wait if you want, but why not? It's just after lunch, so people will be busy. There probably won't be anyone on the roof. Unless you'd rather have someone there? I can call your brother."

Cam shook his head. "I already have enough with you hovering over me like a mother hen. I don't need my brother to be here, too." He took a deep breath, then held his arms out. "I'm ready. We can go whenever you want."

Rocco was extremely careful. While it was true that Cam wasn't hooked up to anything, he was in a lot of pain, and he did have a catheter. Rocco didn't want to cause him even more pain, but he knew it wasn't realistic. Every movement seemed to hurt Cam, but he didn't protest. Instead, he gritted his teeth and hooked his arms around Rocco's neck as soon as he was in Rocco's arms.

Rocco started moving. He made sure to keep a relaxed and steady pace so his movements wouldn't hurt Cam even more. He felt it when Cam finally relaxed, and he hoped it meant that Cam wasn't in as much pain as he'd been earlier.

He was grateful they didn't encounter anyone on their way to the roof. He wanted this moment to himself, but most of all, he wanted *Cam* to have a moment only for himself. He knew some of assassins and mates would fuss over Cam the way Rocco had been doing, and that was obviously the last thing Cam wanted. Rocco wanted to give him exactly what he needed, even though most of the time, he didn't know what that was.

He did this time. Cam didn't want people to hover. He wanted some fresh air. So Rocco was doing his best to give that to him.

It wasn't easy to navigate the stairs, and even worse, the

doors, with Cam in his arms, but Rocco managed. He still went slowly, especially when he had to open doors. He felt Cam wince and whimper a few times, and he resisted the urge to hold him even closer. Cam was in his arms, which was as close as they could be right now, and no doubt for a long while.

Rocco's body was reacting to his mate's closeness. It was easy to ignore, though, especially when Rocco thought about what Cam had been and was still going through. Even if Cam ever wanted to be with Rocco—something Rocco wasn't convinced of just yet—it would be a while before they could bond. It would probably be even longer before they could get in bed together, and again, there was no guarantee it would happen. Rocco wanted Cam desperately, but he needed Cam to be okay and happy even more.

If that meant that he wasn't with Rocco, then Rocco would have to get used to the idea.

"Where the hell is this roof?" Cam asked with a whine.

"We're almost there." Rocco climbed a few more steps, but it apparently wasn't enough to satisfy Cam.

"How big is this place anyway?" he asked. "We passed one door already. I thought we'd arrived."

"Not yet. There are several floors, since everyone lives here. We needed a lot of bedrooms."

Cam grimaced. "And isn't it a problem for you? I mean, the living altogether. I know I'd go crazy if I had to live with my brother twenty-four seven."

Rocco chuckled. "It's not that hard. The warehouse is big enough that we all have our own space, which is the most important thing. There's always someone coming and going, but we're a family. We sometimes fight, but most of the time, we're okay."

And Rocco hoped that Cam would be okay with them, too. He wanted Cam to stay even after he was healed. They hadn't talked about it, and it would take a while for them to do that and for Cam to make his decision. In the meantime, Rocco would hope, and he would pray, even though he wasn't sure he believed there was anything up there that was looking down at them and rooting for them.

Cam hated the infirmary, but he'd never realized just how bad things were until he finally left it. Even the hallway and the stairs were an improvement, and he felt himself relax, even though it wasn't consciously. He leaned harder against Rocco's chest, briefly closing his eyes and taking in a deep breath.

He was free.

He was also in fucking pain, but then, he'd been in pain since what felt like forever, and he was used to it.

"We're almost there," Rocco murmured.

Cam nodded and leaned his cheek against Rocco's shoulder. No matter how many times Cam yelled at him and told him to fuck off, Rocco was always there for him. He was taking care of him, and even though Cam couldn't admit it, it meant a lot. It would have been easy for Rocco to give Cam over to one of the twins. They were the ones doing the healing, after all. All Rocco did was be there for Cam and check on the wounds when he had to. He didn't have to be there and hold Cam's hand through this. Yet that was what he was doing, and Cam couldn't help but feel like he should be more grateful.

He *was* grateful, of course, to Rocco and the assassins, to the council, and of course, his brother. He knew that without them, he would still be in that lab. He might even be dead. That was where he'd been headed when Ox had found him. Instead, he had a second chance at life. He was free.

Except he wasn't, not really. He might not be locked in the

lab anymore, and he might not be experimented on and injured every day, but he was still a prisoner to the pain and the memories. There was no way he would ever be able to forget what had been done to him, and he couldn't help but wonder if it would influence his entire life. Would he ever be able to be with Rocco the way mates should be? Or would he find himself pushing Rocco away, needing more space, wanting to be alone? Cam didn't have an answer to that, but he wished he did. Rocco didn't deserve what Cam was giving him. Rocco would never push, though. It wasn't the kind of man he was. If Cam never wanted to be with him, then Rocco would accept that without protesting.

It was touching, yet painful. Cam realized that the only reason he and Rocco weren't together was him. He didn't even know if he wanted that to change. He wanted to be happy, but right now, he wasn't sure that was in the cards for him. He'd been through too much. He didn't know if he ever would be able to heal, and Rocco deserved much more than a broken man as his mate.

"Here we are," Rocco murmured.

Cam opened his eyes just as Rocco got the roof door open. Sunlight streamed into the staircase, and Cam had to close his eyes again because they hurt. The infirmary was always lit, but it wasn't the same. This was direct sunlight, and it was warm on Cam's skin. He tilted his face up, and he couldn't help the smile that bloomed on his face.

This was freedom. He wasn't stuck in a bed anymore. He didn't have to stay in one place and hope and wonder if he would ever have this again. He *did* have it now.

"There's a couch and some armchairs there in the corner," Rocco said. "If you're okay with that, I'm going to set you down on the couch."

Cam had to admit, at least to himself, that he was more than fine in Rocco's arms. Still, he knew that Rocco couldn't just keep carrying him. Besides, he wasn't sure he wanted Rocco to understand how important this was to him yet.

"All right."

The pain was manageable until Rocco put Cam down. Those movements made all of Cam's bones rattle, and his chest tightened. The scar burned, and Cam gritted his teeth against the pain. He didn't want to cry out. He thought he'd done a good job hiding the pain until Rocco leaned away. He was frowning, and he looked worried. Cam didn't want him to be, though. Rocco was still Cam's doctor, but they weren't in the infirmary anymore, and this almost felt like a date.

He stretched himself out on the couch as much as he could, then patted the armchair close by. "Why don't you sit with me?" he asked.

Rocco's brows shot up. "I thought you'd want some time to yourself."

"Maybe, but I also like talking to you. Sit with me. At least until I feel better."

Rocco frowned and opened his mouth, no doubt to ask Cam how he was feeling, but to Cam's surprise, he snapped it shut and obeyed, sitting in the armchair.

Then he was silent.

Cam wasn't sure how to change that. He wasn't even sure what he wanted. He cleared his throat. "How long have you been a doctor?" he asked.

Rocco seemed surprised at the question. "About ten years. Probably a bit more than that. It just seems like time goes by more slowly when I can't leave the warehouse that much."

Cam frowned. "Why can't you leave?"

Rocco shook his head. "It's not like I *can't*. It's that I don't. I always have to be on hand just in case someone gets hurt."

Cam understood that, but it still didn't make sense. He could see Rocco didn't want to talk about it, though. He looked like he didn't want to talk about himself at all, which was both a relief and dismaying.

"What about the assassins? Can you tell me about them? And about the mates?" That was one of the things Cam was interested in. He and Rocco were mates, even though so far, they hadn't interacted as though they were. Rocco was a doctor, not an assassin, but Cam wanted to know how the mates dealt with everything.

Rocco smiled and relaxed, obviously relieved that the conversation was turned away from him. "What do you want to know about them?"

"I'm not sure. Just tell me."

So Rocco did, and Cam listened. It was nice to listen to Rocco's voice droning on, and Cam was pretty sure that eventually, he would fall asleep. He didn't want to, but he was exhausted, even though he hadn't done anything. He wanted to enjoy the moment. He didn't know when and if Rocco would take him out again, and he didn't want to fall asleep in the middle of it.

So he listened, sending names and jobs and everything he could to memory. He didn't know if he would stay here once he was healed. He had to admit, at least to himself, that it would be a while before he could go back to a normal life and that he was afraid of the unknown waiting for him once he could. Then, something Rocco said made him frown. "Wait. You said that you've known Roark for thirty years," he said.

Roark nodded. "I have."

"But you've only been the doctor here for ten years."

Roark looked away. "I was an assassin before I became a doctor."

"But you're not an assassin anymore."

Rocco shook his head. "I'm not. I haven't been in years. I'm retired."

Cam found it amusing. He had no idea how old Rocco was, but like most shifters, he aged slowly, and he didn't look anywhere near the age of retirement. "Why did you retire?"

The transformation was incredible. Rocco had been fairly relaxed while he talked about the others, but he'd started tensing when the conversation had gone back to him. Now that Cam had asked him a direct question about it, his back went ramrod straight, and his smile faded from his lips. "We should go back inside. You probably need rest."

Cam's first instinct was to protest, but he knew better. He couldn't deny he was tired and that he could use a nap, but most of all, he didn't want to make his mate uncomfortable. He might not have any idea of what he wanted from Rocco, but he did know that he didn't want to hurt his mate. Rocco had been so gentle with him, so nice, even when Cam had been cursing him and telling him to leave him alone. The least Cam could do was not push him when Rocco didn't want to talk about it. "You're right. I could use a nap."

Rocco looked at Cam like he couldn't quite believe that Cam had agreed, but he didn't add anything. Instead, he gathered Cam into his arms again and headed downstairs.

Even with the pain, Cam couldn't help but wonder what had happened. It was evident that whatever the reason behind Rocco's retirement, it was important, and that he didn't want to think about it, let alone talk about it, even with his mate.

It was a mystery, and Cam enjoyed mysteries. He had to be careful, though. He knew that Rocco might never tell him what was going on, and even if he did, it would only be once they trusted each other. That wouldn't happen until Cam let Rocco in, and he wasn't sure he could, not now, and maybe not ever.

CHAPTER THREE

Rocco didn't know what else to do for Cam. He knew he should be doing more. Taking care of Cam's body was one thing, and it was something Rocco was good at, but there was nothing he could do for Cam's mental health. That was going to be a problem soon. Cam was healing, and even though he was still in pain, it wouldn't last forever. And once he was healed, he'd still need help. Rocco knew Cam had nightly nightmares, and it was obvious from the way he reacted to some things that there was a lot of pain and fear in him. Rocco wanted to help, but how? He wasn't a psychologist. He didn't know how to deal with PTSD, even though he'd had it and its effects still lingered. He was pretty sure that was what Cam had, and he hated it.

He might not be able to do anything, but someone else could. A psychologist worked with a few of the assassins, so he knew about them. They'd all been through so much that they needed help. Rocco had never talked to him, not wanting to tell anyone his secret, but he knew Gentry well enough. He'd talked to him a few times, and while he wasn't sure he trusted the man, he knew that Cam needed him.

And he was ready to do anything for Cam, even reach out to someone he didn't trust.

He took a deep breath, then picked up his phone from the desk. He knew Gentry's number because Gentry had given him a business card. Even though Gentry only took care of the mind, he and Rocco had spoken a few times, and Rocco was pretty sure Gentry had realized something was going on with him. He hadn't pushed, but he'd given Rocco his number, and so far, Rocco hadn't used it.

He was about to, but not for himself.

He dialed the number from the business card, then waited.

"Hello?"

"Doctor Reddings?"

"It is, but this is my personal number."

Of course it was. Rocco should have dialed the one *stamped* on the business card, but he'd wanted to make sure to reach Gentry. Since Gentry had written his number on the card, he'd used that one.

He cleared his throat. "This is Rocco. I work for the council as a doctor. I live with a few of your patients." Rocco didn't want to say too much, just in case Gentry wasn't alone. Besides, he wouldn't put it past some people to be listening in, and that was the last thing he needed.

"Of course. I remember you. I gave you both my business card and my personal number."

"You did."

"Have you changed your mind, then?"

"I don't need therapy, if that's what you're asking. I'm calling about one of my patients."

"Give me a moment."

Rocco listened as Gentry quietly spoke to someone. He knew next to nothing about the man, but he was pretty sure that someone had told him that he was mated with two guys. Not that Rocco cared. Gentry could be mated to the Pope as far as he was concerned, and it wouldn't change a thing for him. As long as Gentry could help Cam, he didn't care who the man was or who he fucked.

He heard Gentry move, a door closed, and then Gentry's voice came back. "All right. I'm alone now. We can talk. Has something happened to one of the assassins?"

It was always strange to hear people who didn't live with

them talk about the assassins. Gentry needed to know about them because he was the one healing their mental wounds and helping them, but still. It wasn't easy to deal with when you were used to being a secret. "Not one of the assassins, no. As far as I know, they're all doing well. None of them has been wounded recently." Julian didn't count. He wasn't an assassin, and he hadn't been wounded in the line of duty anyway.

"Good. What can I help you with, then?"

Rocco hesitated. He knew Gentry needed all the details so he could help, but he and Cam hadn't talked about telling other people they were mates. Rocco wasn't sure Cam would want him to, but if it helped, Gentry should probably know it. "It's about my mate."

"I didn't know you'd found your mate. Congratulations. Although since you're telling me about him, I guess there's a problem?"

"There is. We found him in one of those labs. I probably shouldn't tell you about this since I'm his doctor, but he was tortured. He went through a lot, and he's having a hard time healing, both physically and mentally. I'm taking care of his body as much as I can, but he has nightmares, and it's obvious he's not doing well."

There was a pause before Gentry asked, "So you're calling me about him. Does he know you're doing this?"

"He doesn't. I haven't talked to him. I just wanted to know if you could come first. I don't know how he'll react to your presence, to be honest. He has a hard time trusting people, including me."

"That's not surprising, considering what you've told me. I can't make any promises at this point, of course. I can't even promise I'll help him. He needs to work with me if he wants that to happen, and since you said he doesn't know you're calling, I don't know how he'll take my presence."

"I know. I just thought I'd ask if you could help."

"Like I said, I can certainly try. It's my job. I'd like to talk to him."

"You'll have to come here. I can't move him. I don't want to risk it."

"It's fine." Gentry was one of the few people not an assassin or a mate who was allowed into the warehouse. Some days, it was easier than sending the assassins his way. It worked well in this case, since Cam couldn't be moved. He was still in too much pain. Even the short trip to the roof had been hard on his body, and he'd slept several hours after Rocco had tucked him back into bed.

"I'll contact Kameron and the council," Gentry said. "I want to clear it with them first, just in case. But as far as I'm concerned, I'm more than ready to help him. Talk to him, though. Make sure it's something he's ready for."

Rocco wasn't looking forward to that. Still, as far as he could see, this was the only way for Cam to get better, so once he and Gentry hung up, he headed to the infirmary. He hadn't wanted to make the phone call where Cam could hear him, and he was glad he hadn't. Still, now he had to talk to Cam, and he wasn't looking forward to it for the first time since he and Cam had met.

What if Cam took this badly? What if he didn't want to talk to Gentry? Rocco knew that in his place, his knee-jerk reaction would be to say no. Cam already hated needing other people to help him. This probably wouldn't be any different, and it could be a problem. But Rocco really couldn't do more for his mate, and he was at a loss.

He quietly walked into the infirmary, relieved when he saw that Cam was on his bed dozing. He needed rest, but he hated sleeping, especially in the infirmary. Rocco hadn't missed that, but he didn't know what to do about it.

He was a doctor, and he was used to making that kind of decision. In Cam's case, though, it wasn't the same. Cam wasn't merely his patient. He was his mate, and that left Rocco confused. He couldn't help but wonder how he was making the decisions when it came to Cam. Was he acting like Cam's doctor, or as he suspected, like Cam's mate? He didn't know, but it did make a difference. He needed to talk to Cam, but more importantly, he needed to help him.

How, though? Was there anything he could do? Or would he eventually lose Cam to the nightmares and the fear? Rocco didn't know, and he wasn't looking forward to finding out. He would, though eventually. That was how life went.

Cam knew Rocco was in the room. He'd heard the door open, and the only reason he hadn't opened his eyes was that he hadn't been sure who was there. He recognized Rocco's footsteps, though. They'd been spending a lot of time together, and he'd gotten used to his presence.

He wasn't sure why Rocco hadn't said anything. He was probably afraid to wake up Cam, and that was sweet. Still, Cam wasn't sleeping, and for the first time since what felt like forever, he actually felt good. Well, good was an overstatement. He felt decent, and not like he was about to die in five seconds. He opened his eyes, already smiling, but the smile faded when he saw the serious expression on Rocco's face. "What happened?" he asked, startling Rocco.

"You're awake?"

Cam rolled his eyes. "Obviously. What's going on?"

Rocco shook his head and sat in one of the chairs next to Cam's bed. That was enough to tell Cam that whatever he was about to say, Cam probably wasn't going to like it.

He was getting used to that, though. Rocco always had a lot of things to say that Cam didn't like, most of them related to Cam's health.

Cam sighed. "Come on. I'm listening."

Rocco bit his lower lip.

It was such a vulnerable gesture that it made Cam's heart soften. Rocco was always afraid to tell him whatever was on his mind, and it was because Cam had been so bad with him. He'd been pushing him away even when Rocco was only trying to help, and he felt guilty. His feelings hadn't changed, though. He might want to see where things with Rocco would go, but he couldn't find it in himself to trust his mate. He hated it, but he couldn't change it.

"I want to do more for you," Rocco eventually said.

Cam blinked at him. "I don't think I understand."

Rocco gestured at the bed Cam was in. "I've been working on healing your body, and you need it. That's not a problem. But I know you have nightmares, and that you want out of this infirmary. I wish I could do more for you, but I don't know how."

Dammit. Rocco was reminding Cam exactly how bad a shape he was in. Cam knew it wasn't on purpose. Rocco was his mate, but he was also his doctor, and he wanted him to recover. Hell, *Cam* wanted to recover. Rocco wasn't wrong. His body was a while away from what it had been before, as was his mind, but he was healing. He was much better than he'd been when he'd arrived, and he knew he owed that to Rocco and the twins. His brother's presence had helped, too.

Cam hated that Rocco felt like he wasn't doing enough because that wasn't the truth. "You don't have to do anything more. I know you've done everything in your power, and that's okay."

Rocco shook his head. "It's *not* enough. You deserve to get better. You deserve to have everything you've ever wanted from life, and I hate that I can't give that to you."

"Don't you see, though? You've given me new hope. You helped me. I might be a long way from going back to what I was before, but I'm so much better than when Ox found me

41

in the lab."

But he wasn't okay. Even he could admit that. He couldn't help it when his gaze shifted to the infirmary door. He hated this place, even with Rocco here with him. He wanted out, but he knew Rocco wouldn't allow it. He wasn't wrong, either. No matter how much Cam hated being here, it was what made the most sense. Rocco needed to have everything on hand in case something happened to him, and that wouldn't be possible if Cam wasn't here.

"When did you last shift?" Rocco asked suddenly.

Cam didn't want to answer that question. Hell, he wished he hadn't heard it. "I don't know."

Cam prayed that Rocco wouldn't push, but of course, Rocco did. "I should have thought about it sooner. Shifting will help your body heal," Rocco said.

Cam looked away from him. He couldn't stand looking at him right now. "Maybe, but I don't think it's a good idea."

"Even if it doesn't help with the healing, you need to keep in touch with your otter. He needs healing just as badly as you do."

He was right. Rocco wasn't just a human doctor. He was used to taking care of shifters, and Cam was a shifter, even though he hadn't shifted in what felt like forever. There was a reason for that, though.

"And since we're talking about this, I'd like you to see a psychologist. I already called a friend of mine, and he agreed to see you if you agree. I'm healing your body, but he'll be able to help heal your mind."

Cam's first instinct was to say no, but he realized he needed it. He had nightmares, and some days, he couldn't stop thinking about what had been done to him. "I'll talk to him," he agreed.

He also wanted to shift, and talking to a psychologist could help with that. The last time he'd shifted had been like being in a horror movie, and he wasn't sure he could go through that again. He knew Rocco wouldn't hurt him like the scientists had, but what his brain and his heart were saying was different. His mind was trying to make him see that he was safe, but his heart was already racing in his chest at the thought of being that vulnerable. The memories were flooding his mind, and he had to make a conscious effort to keep them away.

"It would help you relax," Rocco continued, apparently not realizing that his words were hurting Cam. "And of course, one of us will be with you when you do it, so we can be sure nothing happens."

Cam shook his head. He wanted to tell Rocco to stop. He wanted Rocco to leave and never bring this up again. He couldn't get the words out, though. They were stuck in his throat, along with the scream that was building in his lungs.

He couldn't shift. Otherwise he would have already, but just the thought made the panic swell in his chest. What would happen to him if he shifted? Even though logically, he knew that Rocco wouldn't hurt him the way the scientists had, he couldn't help the fear. He didn't want to feel like this. He hated that in a way, he'd lost his otter. He wanted to heal, and he suspected Rocco wasn't wrong when he said that shifting could help with that.

But he didn't even want to try. Just the thought made him want to run away, and he would have if he hadn't been stuck in bed.

"Cam?"

Cam felt Rocco's hands on his arms, and he jerked away, trying to scramble off the bed. Of course, even though he wasn't hooked to monitors or anything else, he was weak, and he almost fell face down from the bed. Luckily for him, Rocco was there. He caught him before he could hurt himself and helped him back on the bed.

"Cam?" he asked, his voice laced with worry.

Cam shook his head. He opened his mouth, but the only thing that came out was a whimper. Instead of answering, Cam curled himself into a ball. It hurt his chest, but he didn't care. He needed this. He needed to protect himself. He needed to make sure that no one would hurt him the way the scientists had. His heart was yelling at him to run, to make sure that Rocco couldn't do what they had done. He didn't know what else to do, so he curled in his bed and tried to breathe as panic made it almost impossible.

Rocco had made things worse. He wasn't sure how, but he could see it from the way Cam was reacting. It would have been obvious even to a blind man, and Rocco wasn't blind.

Cam had curled in on himself and was hiding under the blanket. Rocco couldn't help but berate himself for it, but making sure Cam was okay was more important, so he reached for him, stopping just before touching him.

What if Cam freaked out because Rocco touched him.? It was the last thing Rocco wanted, so instead, he crouched closer to the bed. "Cam?" he asked. Cam whimpered. That was his only answer, and Rocco was starting to panic, too. "You don't have to shift if you don't want to," he murmured, trying to keep his voice as soft and gentle as possible. "It was just an idea."

Cam didn't react, and Rocco didn't stop speaking, hoping it would help. "I do think it will help you, but I understand you don't want to, and I'm not going to push. I would never force you to do anything, including shifting. Come on, sweetheart. Talk to me and try to relax. Please." Rocco didn't want to give Cam sedatives since Cam didn't like them, but if he had to, he would. He wanted to do what Cam wanted, but his health was more important right now.

Taking a risk, Rocco put a hand on Cam's back. When Cam didn't push him away, he stroked his hand up and down in, what he hoped was a soothing gesture. He almost smiled when Cam finally relaxed under his palm, but he knew they weren't out of the woods yet. He waited, praying that Cam would explain what was happening. He needed to know what not to say or do ever again.

"I can't shift," Cam finally said.

Rocco frowned. "You can't? I'm pretty sure that nothing the scientists did to you blocked your shift."

Cam's face finally popped out of the blanket, and of course, he was scowling at Rocco. "I'm sure that I could if I wanted to, but I *can't*," he repeated. "You know what they did to me when I was shifting. You saw the result."

Shit. Of course that was the problem. How could Rocco not have realized that sooner? Cam had been tortured while he'd been shifting. It made sense that he didn't even want to think about doing it right now. Rocco probably wouldn't, either, if he were in his place.

Rocco sat back into the chair and rubbed his face. "I'm so sorry, Cam. I didn't think."

Cam snorted. "That's obvious."

Rocco peeked at him, relieved to see that Cam seemed to be doing better already. "I should have. I am really, *really* sorry." He couldn't believe what he'd done. What if he'd made Cam's recovery even harder? What if he'd pushed Cam to go too far and too soon? He would never forgive himself.

Cam's shoulders shuddered, and Rocco wondered if he was crying. If he'd done that, well, he wasn't sure what he would do, but he was already berating himself.

Then, he realized that Cam was laughing, not crying. "Are you okay?" he asked.

Cam shook his head and tried to sit up, but it was still hard for him, so Rocco helped him. He didn't miss the grimace of pain, but it was gone as fast as it had appeared.

"We're a well-suited couple, aren't we?" Cam asked.

Rocco didn't know what he was talking about. "We are?"

Cam shrugged. "You're my doctor. I'm in so much freaking pain that some days, I wish it would just *end*. You're trying to help me, but I'm not letting you. Instead, I freaked out so badly that I made you freak out, too."

Rocco bounced his knee. He wanted to insist, but it hadn't gone well the first time. "I stand by what I said," he eventually said. Cam's eyes widened, and Rocco rushed to finish. "I do think that shifting would do you good. It would help your body heal, and it might take away some of the pain. It would also help you relax more. You could take a nap in your otter form. I won't force you, of course. But if you ever decide that you want to do it, I'll be there when you do. I hope you know by now that I won't hurt you. I would rather kill myself before I do anything like that. If you trust me enough to shift while I'm there, if you're able to get over the memories and the pain, I'll make sure nothing happens to you."

Cam frowned. "Will you shift, too?" The frown deepened. "I don't think I've ever asked you what you shift into. You know I'm an otter, of course, but I don't know about you."

That was easy to answer. "I'm a jerboa shifter."

Cam's eyes widened. "Really? That's a rodent, right? The one with long legs."

"Really. So you see that I wouldn't be a danger to you even in my shifted form. Hell, considering how much bigger I am than you in our human form, I'm probably more dangerous to you right now than I would be if we shifted."

"You seem to be trying hard to make me understand that you *could* hurt me," Cam pointed out.

Dammit. Rocco was making a mess of things, wasn't he? He rubbed the back of his neck and thought before opening his mouth again. "I understand where you're coming from. I might not have been through what you've been through, but I spent some time in a lab, too. I was experimented on. I wouldn't have become a council assassin otherwise. I might be retired, but that doesn't mean that the ability the scientists gave me is gone. So I know where you're coming from. I can understand it, and I understand the fear. I would never push you to do something you're not feeling up to, and I'm sorry if I scared you."

Cam's shoulders slumped. "But you still think I should do it."

"I do. Like I said, I understand how hard it is. But the lab already robbed you of so much. Do you want to allow the scientists to rob you of the pleasure of being an otter shifter, too? You don't have to shift if you don't feel up to it. You haven't until now, and it won't change anything. I do think it would be good for you, but it's not indispensable for your recovery. Still, it's something you should think about. I can't make any promises except that I will be there and keep you safe, and I hope you trust me enough by now. It's okay if you don't, though." Rocco hated the thought, but he understood.

It had taken him so long to trust people after he'd run away from the lab. Even after Win and the council had taken him in, he hadn't let anyone close to him for months. Win had finally managed to break through, but even that had been hard.

Rocco wasn't entirely healed, and he knew it. Some days, he still had nightmares about the lab, and about the past in general. He wished he could make sure it wouldn't happen to Cam, but he knew better. He knew what Cam had been through, and all he wanted was for him to make it out of the nightmare he was still living in. He wanted to do everything he could to help his mate, but he already had. This was the last attempt, and Rocco hoped Cam would realize he needed to do this. He hoped Cam would understand that he couldn't allow the scientists to take this away from him, too.

But he'd said what he had to say about it. Now the ball was on Cam's side, and he was the one who needed to make the decision. Whatever that decision was, Rocco would be there for him, though. He would always be there for his mate, even if Cam never wanted him the same way he wanted Cam.

Cam wanted to trust Rocco. He could see that Rocco was distraught about what had happened, and with everything they'd said to each other since Cam had arrived at the warehouse, he knew Rocco hadn't meant to hurt him.

Still, the result was what it was. Even though Rocco hadn't meant anything by it, Cam had panicked. He still had the taste of panic in his mouth, and it made him want to throw up, especially after Rocco explained that he truly thought that Cam should do it.

And Cam wanted to.

Rocco wasn't wrong when he said Cam couldn't allow the lab to take this from him, too. Cam hated that even the thought of shifting made him panic. He was a shifter. Doing that should be as natural as breathing to him, yet since he'd left the lab, he hadn't done it. His otter wasn't happy with him, but thankfully, it understood. It was healing, too.

Would shifting help both Cam and his otter? Cam couldn't help but wonder, and he also couldn't help but wonder if he could do it. He wanted to. He wanted to be strong enough to show the scientists that they hadn't broken him. He wasn't sure that he wasn't broken, though. He wasn't sure of anything right now. He didn't even know if he could trust Rocco.

His brain knew that Rocco would never hurt him. It didn't even have anything to do with the fact that they were mates. Rocco was a doctor. He didn't hurt people. He might have been an assassin before, but he wasn't anymore, and the assassins weren't bad people anyway. They only killed people who deserved it, and that was fine with Cam, especially after what had happened to him.

Cam sucked in a breath. It was easier to breathe now, and he was relieved. Still, he needed to give Rocco an answer. He didn't want to hurt his mate.

"Okay," he started. Rocco's eyes widened, and Cam put a hand up. If he was going to do this, if he was going to force himself to shift even though the thought alone made him want to run away, he wanted something in exchange. "I *will* shift, but only if I'm allowed to leave the infirmary permanently after that."

Rocco's smile vanished as if it had never been there. "You know why you can't leave the infirmary."

Cam crossed his arms over his chest. "I know that you don't want me to leave. You want to keep an eye on me. You want to make sure I'm okay. And that's fine. I still need medical attention. But I'm feeling better, and I don't think I need to be stuck here anymore. I haven't had an emergency for weeks, and the only thing you've been doing is watching me like a hawk. You can do that and everything you might need to do somewhere else."

"The infirmary is safer if something does happen."

Cam swallowed. He would have to explain why he wanted out, wouldn't he? He didn't want to, but Rocco probably deserved to know. "I hate being here," he quietly said. "It reminds me of the lab. It has the same smells, and even though I know you won't hurt me, the thought is always there in the back of my mind. I need out of this place. I'm not saying that I want to leave the warehouse, just that I want a bedroom. I want to be away from hospital beds. I want to be away from the smell of disinfectant. Please." Cam was begging, and he didn't even care. Now that the words were out, he needed Rocco to say yes.

His heart was racing in his chest, and he was already

sweating at the thought of shifting, but if it meant being free, then he would do it. He would have to. He couldn't go back, not when freedom was so close.

Rocco took his time answering. He never did anything on impulse, not when it came to his job. Cam knew Rocco wanted him to be safe, and asking that of him was a big step. He could say no, but Cam prayed he wouldn't. Rocco might think that shifting would help him, but Cam suspected that leaving the infirmary would help him even more. He hoped he would sleep better and that, in turn, would make it easier to rest, eat, and heal.

Rocco slowly nodded. "All right."

Cam had to be sure he'd heard that right. "*All right?* You mean I can leave the infirmary?"

"You can. I should probably have realized the problem sooner. It was stupid of me not to."

Cam shook his head, relieved. "You couldn't have known. I've never told anyone."

Rocco's smile was sad. "I wish you'd told me. I would have found a way to get you out of here sooner. But you're right. You're not hooked up to anything, and we'll probably be able to take out the catheter soon. You can try to go back to a normal life. In fact, you *should* try it. So I'll find you a bedroom." He hesitated. "I need to be able to check in on you often, though."

"That's fine. I don't care, as long as I'm out of here." Cam swallowed. "I'm ready."

Rocco shook his head. "You don't have to shift. I know I made it sound like you had to in order to leave this place, but you don't. I'm not going to force you to do something you're not comfortable with. Leaving the infirmary doesn't have anything to do with you shifting. You can go even if you don't."

It was a relief, but now that the thought had been put in Cam's mind, he wanted to do it. "You were right. I shouldn't let the scientists take this away from me, too. I don't want to let them. Besides, what better place to shift than here? At least if something goes wrong, you'll be there to help."

"Of course I will. I'll do anything you need me to do, starting with taking the catheter out now if you want to do this."

Cam nodded, then closed his eyes. He could feel his otter there, just under the surface, already pushing to come out. His palms were sweaty, and he rubbed them against the sheet. He could do this. He had to. "Take it out."

While Rocco did that, Cam focused on his otter again. The last time he'd shifted, his chest had been open wide. The scientists had been staring at what happened to the inside of his body, and it had hurt so much. He was terrified of feeling that kind of pain again, even though he knew it wouldn't happen. It had never hurt when he shifted, not until the scientists had put their hands on him.

This was natural for him. It wouldn't hurt because it *was* him.

Cam felt Rocco step away, but he didn't open his eyes. He had to stay focused. He wouldn't be able to do it otherwise.

He jerked when he felt fingers on his thigh, but he was also grateful for them. He grabbed Rocco's hand and linked their fingers together, then took a deep breath.

He didn't shift. He had to take more deep breaths to steady his heart, and his otter helped, even though Cam could feel how excited it was at finally coming out to play.

So he shifted.

Once he started the process, it was easy, as easy as breathing. His otter came out, exploding out of the hospital gown he was wearing. It didn't need that much space, but he didn't want to be covered with anything, not right now, not when he was already covered with fur.

Cam smiled. The fear was gone. He'd done it, and he was okay. He was still in pain, but that was because of the wound and the scars. It would pass, eventually. In the meantime, though, he'd freed himself from the lab and the scientists.

He opened his eyes. Rocco was beaming at him, and Cam showed him his teeth. It made Rocco laugh, and Cam felt better. He should have trusted Rocco sooner. Rocco knew what he was doing. He was a doctor, but like he'd said before, he'd also been in a lab. He knew better than a lot of people what Cam was going through.

"Will you be okay?" Rocco asked.

Cam nodded. He wasn't feeling like his old self, but he was closer to it than he'd been ten minutes earlier. The fear, the pain, the wariness, all of that was still there, but it was easier to deal with them.

"How about I shift, too?" Rocco asked.

Cam blinked at him, then nodded. He wanted to see his mate's animal form. He wanted them to have this together. He didn't know when—or if—he and Rocco would ever feel this close again. He hoped so, but he couldn't make any kind of promises. He wanted this with him, though.

He watched as Rocco took off his clothes. He didn't seem to be ashamed of his body, and he didn't have a reason to be. He was gorgeous, and Cam found himself hoping that eventually, he would be able to welcome Rocco in his life as his mate. Now wasn't the time to think about that, though. Instead, he focused on Rocco's jerboa form as soon as he shifted.

He wished they were Nix and that they could talk in each other's mind, but they were only shifters. Instead of talking, they curled around each other, and Cam couldn't help but smile when Rocco settled against him. He was smaller, but he was a protector, hooking his tail over Cam's stomach and pushing against him. And he was cute, with long legs and big ears, and of course, his tail.

It was easier to relax this way. Cam closed his eyes, relieved at feeling Rocco's furry body against him. Rocco hadn't hurt him. Cam hadn't expected him to, but it helped to realize just how bad he'd been when it came to Rocco.

He could trust his mate. He'd been pushing everyone away because he was afraid, even though he knew no one would hurt him. He'd stopped living, and that meant that the scientists had won.

Cam hated all that. If he could shift, he could live on. He could find his way to happiness again. It wouldn't be easy, but the first step was to trust people, especially people who were showing him he could trust them through their actions. It was talking to Ox and explaining what was going on. It was letting Rocco into his life.

It wouldn't be easy, but Cam could do it. He was sure of it. If he could shift even after what had been done to him the last time he had, then he could do anything.

CHAPTER FOUR

When Cam had asked to move out of the infirmary, Rocco hadn't been sure *where* to move him. There were a few empty guest rooms, but he didn't want to think of Cam alone there. Of course, he'd known Cam wouldn't be alone. Ox had visited him a few times already, as had Dasha.

But Rocco hadn't moved Cam into a guestroom. Instead, he'd moved him into his bedroom. He wasn't sure Cam knew that. They hadn't talked about it, but Rocco's jerboa felt better knowing Cam was in their territory. Cam might be angry when he found out, but Rocco supposed he would find out once that happened. In the meantime, Cam seemed to be doing okay, which was all Rocco wanted.

The fear was still there. Even though Cam had been okay for a while already, Rocco couldn't help but wonder if he would stay that way. What if something happened? What if he needed to be in the infirmary? But it was a moot point to think about that. If something did happen, then Rocco would do everything he could to make sure Cam was okay.

"Where have you been sleeping?" Ox asked.

Once again, Rocco hadn't heard him coming. He pasted a smile on his face and turned to face his brother-in-law. He and Cam might not be together, but that didn't change that fact. "Good evening to you, too," he said.

Ox rolled his eyes. "Good evening. Now, where have you been sleeping.?"

"I don't think it's any of your business."

Ox crossed his arms over his chest. "You're right. It's not.

But I don't think Cam knows that he's sleeping in your bedroom, and maybe he ought to."

Rocco sighed. He should have known Ox would give him problems. He was overprotective of his brother, and Rocco couldn't blame him. Who wouldn't be after what had happened to Cam? "Again, I don't think it's any of your business. I've been sleeping in the infirmary, though."

Ox grimaced. "I guess there are more than enough beds there. Why are you doing this, though?"

Rocco shrugged. He didn't have an answer—he'd acted on instinct. When Cam had decided he wanted out of the infirmary, the solution had sprung up in Rocco's mind, and he hadn't paused to think about it. "He's my mate. I want him close."

"I understand that. You should probably tell him, though. I have nothing against you, Rocco, but I don't want my brother to be involved in something he doesn't realize he's involved in. He's your mate. Talk to him."

Ox made it sound easy, but he and Dasha hadn't had the same problems Rocco and Cam did. Even though they'd had their own problems, especially coming from Ox, it wasn't the same. Rocco was terrified he was going to lose Cam. They hadn't talked about being mates, not beyond that first time when they'd realized it. What if Cam didn't want Rocco? What if he hated that he was sleeping in Rocco's bedroom? Rocco supposed he would find out eventually, but he wanted a little reprieve. Was that too much to ask for?

Maybe.

He turned back to the tray he was putting together for Cam. Cam might not be in the infirmary anymore, but he still didn't have an easy time walking around, so this was easier and faster. He'd grumbled a few times about it, but Rocco had already given in a lot. He wouldn't give when it came to this. He'd been clear, and Cam had relented—for now.

Ox sighed and patted Rocco's shoulder. "I just want my brother to be happy, and you, too. Talk to him. I know things aren't easy right now, but you know as well as I do that if you ever want a relationship with Cam, you're going to have to tell him about this. Don't wait until you don't have a way out and until it looks like you only confessed because you had to. I know Cam. He won't be happy if he feels you're lying to him."

Rocco already knew that, but he forced himself to focus on something else while he got the tray ready. The assassins were talking, and while Rocco didn't usually keep up with what they were doing, it was important to him to know that the people who'd put Cam in the lab were paying.

"How many are there left?" Armand asked.

He and Roark were at the dining table with their heads close together as they looked over a piece of paper. It was a list of the government officials who'd known about the lab. They'd created it, had funded it, and had been okay with what was happening inside. If Rocco had his way, he would kill them himself, but there was no way he was leaving the warehouse, not with Cam still here.

"A few. We're having a hard time locating this one. He probably knows what's going on, and he's making sure we can't get to him."

"I'll take care of him. I can find him."

Armand probably could. He could shift into other human beings, and that meant that most of the time, the people he was sent to kill didn't even realize something was wrong until he killed them. Rocco didn't like the idea of not making those people suffer, but at least they wouldn't hurt anyone else.

Still, he felt like he wasn't doing enough in this case, too. Cam was still recovering, even though it was weeks since he'd been freed from the lab. What had been done to him was horrific, and Rocco wanted the people who'd hurt him to be in as much pain as he had been.

In as much pain as he still was.

He *was* recovering, but slowly. Rocco was doing everything he could, but he was only human. Cam was, too. There would be no miracles, not in this case.

Rocco took the tray and headed upstairs. He nodded at a few people who smiled at him, but he was grateful when none of them tried to stop him. He didn't want to talk. He wanted to get this to Cam and to spend some time with him. He knew Ox was right and that eventually, he would have to explain that Cam was sleeping in his bedroom while he'd moved to the infirmary, but not now. Hopefully, not for a while.

Rocco hadn't noticed that Ox had left the kitchen, so he was surprised when he got to his bedroom and found Ox there, the door open, the brothers talking. He paused, wondering if Ox had told Cam about it, but he knew better. No one would tell Cam, not even Ox, even though Cam was his brother. He knew he shouldn't intervene between mates, no matter the situation. Still, Rocco knew he was right. He wouldn't be this terrified if Ox weren't.

Since neither the brothers had noticed Rocco, he took a moment to look at them. In the beginning, Cam had been okay with people. After only a few hours, though, he'd closed off, and he'd stayed that way for too long. Rocco understood why. He was terrified that someone was going to hurt him, and even though he knew he could trust Rocco and Ox and everyone else in the house, it was hard to resist the part of him that told him he needed to hide and make sure no one could get their hands on him.

But that was changing. Rocco didn't know if it was because Cam was healing or because he was finally out of the infirmary, but he couldn't remember seeing Cam so lively.

He was talking with Ox, his arms moving in front of him. Rocco looked at him, noticing a few winces as he moved, but apart from that, he seemed to be fine.

Calling Gentry had been a good idea. Rocco suspected it was a mix of things—Cam talking with Gentry, but also being out of the infirmary and healing, were allowing him to take a step forward to living his life. Shifting had probably helped, too.

Cam looked up and smiled when he saw Rocco standing there. "Did you bring me dinner?" he asked.

Rocco didn't have to fake a smile this time. He stepped into the bedroom and held up the tray. "Exactly. I hope you're hungry."

The smile on Cam's face widened. "I'm starving."

Cam was happy to see Rocco, and he was even happier to see the tray in Rocco's hands. He was starving, and he hadn't felt like that in a long time. It had been a few days since he'd left the infirmary, and he was finally looking forward to eating.

He raised his hands and wiggled his fingers. "What did you bring me?" he asked as Rocco stepped into the bedroom and handed the tray to him.

"Lasagna."

Cam beamed. "I love lasagna." And he could finally enjoy it again. God, he'd thought he couldn't, not after what he'd been through. He'd thought he was done living.

He'd been wrong.

Ox patted Cam's thigh. "I'm going to leave you to your dinner."

"You can stay," Cam said, and they were both aware of the fact that he wouldn't have said that only a few days earlier.

Cam wasn't sure what it was. Probably a mix of his body healing, talking to the psychologist Rocco had found for him, leaving the infirmary, but most of all, realizing that he could trust Rocco and that he had stopped living even though he was very much alive.

He didn't want the lab and the scientists to have any kind of hold on him ever again, so he was forcing himself to see the good in his life. He was still in pain, and he probably would be for a while, but he was free. He was healing. He had his brother, and he'd met his mate. What more could he want? Of course, if he had his way, he would be in much better shape, but that would come. He was as happy as he could be considering the situation, and that was enough, at least for now.

Ox shook his head. "I promised Dasha I'd eat with him."

That was different, too. Before Cam had been taken, he and Ox had been close, more like best friends than brothers. They were still close, but now, Cam had to deal with the fact that Ox had met his mate. He wasn't the most important person in Ox's life anymore. Dasha was, and even though it was weird, it was okay. It was how things should be. Cam knew he was the most important person in Rocco's life, even though Rocco hadn't said anything about it. Eventually, they would need to talk, but for now, this was enough.

"Come and find me tomorrow," he told Ox.

Ox leaned forward and kissed the top of Cam's head. "Of course. You couldn't keep me away even if you tried."

"I'm not going to try. I want to talk to you. I've missed you."

Ox's expression softened. "I've missed you, too."

Cam knew it had been mostly his fault if they weren't as close, but hopefully, that was changing.

Ox left, but Rocco didn't. Instead, he took the second plate from the tray and settled into an armchair in the corner of the room.

Cam looked around. He'd had a lot of time to examine the room since he'd already been here a few days, and he'd come to a conclusion. He wanted to check if he was right. "This is a nice bedroom," he said, trying to sound innocent.

Rocco's fork stopped moving. "It is."

"Are all guestrooms this nice?"

Rocco cleared his throat. "They're very nice, yes."

"It sounds a bit weird. I mean, how many guests do the assassins have? It can't be a lot."

Cam knew he'd been right when Rocco looked away. He felt guilty, and that much was obvious on his face. Cam had to resist the urge to smile. He wanted to hear where this was going.

"We don't have a lot of them, but as you know, we keep finding mates. Sometimes, they need their own room, especially when there's something going on with them like there is with you."

Cam slowly nodded. "I see. Still, this one looks like someone's been living in it. I didn't take someone's bedroom, did I?"

"Of course not. Don't worry about that."

Cam smiled. "I'm not worried. What about you? Where have you been sleeping?"

Rocco froze. He looked like a deer in headlights, and Cam *knew* he'd been right. "I've been sleeping, don't worry," he said.

He was trying not to tell the truth while also not lying to Cam.

Cam shook his head. "I'm just wondering where you've been sleeping, because it's obvious that this is your bedroom," he finally said.

Rocco sighed, and his shoulders slumped. "You're right. This *is* my bedroom." There was a hint of pink on his cheeks, and Cam found it utterly adorable. He probably shouldn't, since Rocco was a grown man, but he couldn't help it.

"What did you do?" Cam asked.

"Nothing. You said you wanted out of the infirmary, and I agreed it was a good idea."

"You didn't have to put me in your bedroom, though. Ox confirmed that there are several empty guestrooms. I could have taken one of those."

"But they're all on the upper floor because they're newer ones. This one is closer to the infirmary, even if it's by only one floor. It's better in case you need something."

"Really?" Cam suspected that was bullshit, but he knew better than to say it out loud. He knew Rocco was still worried about his health, as any good doctor would be. The fact that they were mates added to the worry, and he wasn't going to bust Rocco's ass for it.

"Of course. I wouldn't lie to you," Rocco said.

Cam arched a brow. "I'm not saying you lied to me, but it was a pretty big omission," he pointed out.

"I can take you to a guest room if you want."

"I don't want to. I'm comfortable here," he said. Rocco visibly relaxed, but Cam wasn't done. "I have a condition, though."

Rocco huffed. "Don't you always? What?"

"I want you to move back into your bedroom."

Rocco blinked. "You want me to move back in here?"

"That's what I just said, isn't it?"

"It is, but there's only one bed, Cam."

Cam looked away. He might be convinced of this, but it was still awkward to talk about it. "There is, and we can share."

There was a pause before Rocco asked, "Are you sure about that?" His voice was soft and gentle, as if he expected rejection and for Cam to change his mind since he had the opportunity to.

Cam wasn't going to, though. "I'm sure. We're both adults, so it shouldn't be a problem to share." That, and they were mates. Even though Cam was nowhere near ready to have sex with Rocco, he wanted more than what they already had. He wanted them to take the next step toward being a couple, and while he had no idea how to make that happen, he supposed that sharing a bed would help. If anything, they would be closer physically, and that couldn't be a bad thing.

"You're still healing," Rocco said.

Cam rolled his eyes. "I know that. I can feel it. I also know it's going to take me a while to fully heal. What does it have to do with sharing a bed?"

"I don't want to hurt you while we're sleeping."

"Why would you?"

"What if I roll over and fall on top of you? What if I bump into you?"

Cam had thought about that, too. "Then I'll wake up and be in pain, and you'll apologize. Are you *trying* to find reasons not to share a bed with me?"

The pink on Rocco's cheeks deepened. "Of course not. I just want to make sure you thought about it and that it's not going to be a problem. I couldn't forgive myself if I did something that pushed your healing back."

"I can't promise you won't, but I think this is part of my healing, too. Come on, Rocco. Please. I know we haven't talked about it, but I trust you. I want more." Cam felt incredibly vulnerable while admitting that, and he had no idea how Rocco would react, but he prayed it would be good. He needed it to be. Now that he was finally living his life again, he wanted more than pain and fear.

He wanted his mate. He wanted Rocco.

Rocco was still hesitant, but how could he say no to Cam? He couldn't. That was the answer.

It looked like he was going to move back into his bedroom after all.

In the meantime, though, he made sure that Cam was

eating. Cam rolled his eyes at him a few times, but he didn't say anything about it, and Rocco settled down. The change in his mate over the past few days had been dramatic, and he couldn't deny that moving Cam out of the infirmary had been a good idea.

Cam was starting to live again. Rocco suspected that shifting had had a lot to do with it, but he hadn't asked, and Cam hadn't volunteered information. Rocco wasn't sure what had happened that day. They shifted, then cuddled on the bed together, but they hadn't talked. Apparently, they hadn't needed to talk. Cam was healing on his own, which was what Rocco had wanted. He'd been afraid he wouldn't be able to do anything more, but that didn't seem to matter. Cam had taken things into his own hands, and Rocco couldn't have been happier.

He wasn't sure how things would work between the two of them now that they were sharing a bed, but it was time to discover that. It wasn't bedtime yet, but it would be soon, and Rocco was nervous. He didn't know what to expect, but he wanted to make Cam happy.

"Have you been thinking about what's next for you?" Rocco asked. He didn't want to push, but he wanted to know if Cam wanted to include him in his future. It sounded like he did, but Rocco needed to be sure.

Cam frowned and blinked at him. "Next?"

"You know. Once you're well enough to leave your bed. I mean, no one will kick you out of the warehouse. You can stay, and I hope you will. What did you want to do with your life before you were taken, though?"

Cam frowned. "Can I be honest with you?"

"Of course you can. I always want you to be honest with me."

Cam nodded. "All right. Then I can tell you that I'm terrified."

Rocco wasn't surprised. He could remember all too well when he'd escaped from the lab. He'd had such a hard time trusting people, and he'd been terrified he would be taken again. "You know we'll protect you," he said.

Cam shrugged. "I know. You, Ox, and everyone else. You won't allow anything to happen to me. I'm aware of that. The fear I feel doesn't have logic. It's just way too easy for me to imagine what would happen if the scientists got their hands on me again."

Rocco's hands tightened into fists. He wanted to find the people who'd hurt Cam and beat them into a pulp. He wanted them to hurt as much as they'd hurt Cam. He wanted to fix things for his mate, but he was starting to realize that he couldn't. No matter how much he wanted to, Cam was the one who had to make decisions, and he was the one who had to work on his fear. He already was, with Gentry, but it would be a while before he could go back to a normal life, or at least, as normal a life as he could have considering everything.

That meant that he needed to heal, both physically and mentally, at his own rhythm, no matter what Rocco wanted or did. Rocco pushing might make things worse and harder.

Rocco should have known it would be better to stick to medical stuff with Cam. He was asking personal questions, and he was messing things up. Why had he decided to move Cam into his bedroom to begin with? He should have known this wouldn't work. He should have realized how dangerous it would be. He was risking Cam's health, and he needed to stop.

"Rocco? What's going on in that head of yours?" Cam asked.

Rocco shook his head. He couldn't tell Cam about this. He hadn't told him about his past, and it was better if he never did.

"Come on," Cam pushed. "I know I can talk to you, but the

same goes for you. You can talk to me if you need to."

"I don't need to talk to anyone. I'm sorry I asked about this. It's your business, and I have no right to know it."

Cam blinked. "What are you talking about?"

"I shouldn't have asked you what you were planning. Like I said, it's your business. I just wanted you to know that you could stay here for as long as you wanted or needed."

Cam put his fork down. "There's something else. You don't have to be afraid to ask me about the future. For the first time in what feels like forever, I finally have a future again. And it's thanks to you."

Rocco shook his head. "It's thanks to *you*. You're the one doing the healing. You're the one working on yourself. I didn't do anything."

"That's not true," Cam snapped.

He sounded angry, and it wasn't something Rocco was used to. "It is. I did everything I could, but you were the one who agreed to see Gentry. You're the one who stood up for yourself. You told me you didn't want to stay in the infirmary, that it brought back bad memories even though you'd never been there before. I should have realized that." That made Rocco a lousy doctor, and he wasn't sure he could afford that since he was also a lousy person. He was terrified to tell Cam about that, though. He *wouldn't* tell Cam about it because he couldn't afford to.

"I don't understand what you're saying," Cam said. He sounded utterly lost, and Rocco hated that he'd been the one to do that to him.

Dammit. He should never have met his mate. He wished Cam *weren't* his mate, almost as much as he was happy that Cam was. What was he supposed to do now? He and Cam had already talked about it. They both knew they were mates, and eventually, Cam would want more than what they had. Not that it would be hard, since they didn't have anything at all.

Rocco should have known better. For Cam's safety, he needed to stay away. He knew Cam wouldn't take that well, though. He was finally starting to live again, and Rocco suspected that he'd want him to be part of his life. It would make sense, but it didn't mean it was the best idea.

Would Cam understand if Rocco told him that, though? Rocco didn't know, and he didn't want to find out. He didn't want to hurt Cam even more than he'd already been hurt, but that was where things were going.

He swallowed. "Did you have any questions regarding your health?" he asked.

Cam opened his mouth, then closed it again. "No. We've already talked about it, and I know everything I need to know. What I want to know is why you're doing this," he said.

Rocco needed to find a way to tell him without actually telling him. "I'm your doctor."

"You are, but you're also my mate," Cam snapped. "Can you stop behaving as if we weren't just talking about sharing a bed?"

Rocco swallowed. "About that."

"Don't say it. Don't you *dare* say that it's not a good idea and that you'll continue sleeping in the infirmary. What happened, Rocco? You changed in just a few seconds, and I don't understand. Did I do something that hurt you? Did I offend you? Because if I did, you should tell me so I won't do it again."

Rocco hated that Cam thought this was his fault when it wasn't. He had no intention of explaining himself, though. He couldn't allow himself to. Cam didn't hate him, but he would if he found out what Rocco had done. They all would, and Rocco would suffer. It was a miracle that Rocco hadn't hurt any of the assassins or the mates, but then that was why he'd stayed away from them. He should have stayed away from Cam, too. Maybe it wasn't too late to do that.

Something was wrong. It was clear as day, but Cam had no idea what. He didn't know what he could do to make everything right again, but it was obvious talking to Rocco and pushing him to admit what was going on in that brain of his wouldn't help.

For a second, it made him wonder if things would be better for him if Rocco *did* stay away. He'd thought about that, too, during his days in Rocco's bedroom, so he already knew the answer. It didn't matter that his fear was trying to take over once again. He would *not* be better off without Rocco. He knew it, and he couldn't allow fear to make him doubt.

Rocco had done so much for him, and Cam would never be able to thank him enough. Right now, Rocco was saying that Cam needed to stay away from him, but Cam had the impression that it was more for Cam's benefit than Rocco's. It didn't make sense, but then, not much in his life made sense these days. He didn't know anything about Rocco's past, only that Rocco had been in a lab and that it was how he'd become a council assassin. What had happened to him in that lab, though? Was he still living through the nightmares and the fear?

It was entirely possible. Gentry had told Cam that Rocco wasn't his patient. He hadn't said anything else, and Cam hadn't pushed. That answer had been enough for him to know that if Rocco still had PTSD from his experience, he wasn't working on it. He wanted Cam to be okay, but it seemed like *he* wasn't okay. Cam didn't know how to help him, and he didn't know if he could, not with everything that was going on. He would find out, though. If there was anyone he owed anything to, it was Rocco.

Besides, Rocco was part of Cam's future, and Cam wanted that future. He didn't know how long it would take him and Rocco to be together as mates, and he wasn't about to rush things. Still, he wanted them to have a chance, and they wouldn't if Rocco pushed him away like he was trying to do right now.

"I know we barely know each other," he said, trying to think about the right words that wouldn't make Rocco bolt or brush him off. "And I know that being mates doesn't mean we're friends or anything like that. I realize you're probably closer to some of the people who live here than you are to me, and that's okay, at least for now. It'll change. But I still want you to know that you can tell me anything. I don't know your past, but you told me enough for me to realize that it was as hard as mine has been. You were in a lab, and it left you permanently scarred. I realize this is probably the last thing you want to think about, but please, don't push me away because of what happened to you. I, better than a lot of people, can understand it. I can accept it, whatever it is."

Rocco chuckled darkly and shook his head. "You can accept it? You sound so sure of that, but you don't even know *what* you would have to accept."

It wasn't the answer Cam had wanted, but it was an answer, and he could deal with it. "How can you know what I can or can't accept if you won't talk to me?" he asked.

"I don't want to tell you. There's a reason no one else knows, so please stop pushing."

Cam didn't want to. He didn't care that Rocco didn't want to talk. Rocco had made sure he talked even when he didn't want to. He'd said it would be easier for Cam to heal if he did, and he'd been right. "Don't you think we should get to know each other?" he asked. "We're mates. That won't change, no matter what we do with that knowledge. How can you know we wouldn't be good together if you don't even want to try?"

Rocco shook his head. "We don't have to try for me to know that I can't be good for you."

That was new. It wasn't unexpected, though. For whatever reason, Rocco seemed to believe that, and he was afraid he would hurt Cam. Cam didn't know why, but he wanted to find out, and more importantly, he wanted Rocco to realize it was bullshit.

A few days before, Cam wouldn't have pushed. Now, though, he was stronger. He realized he was still at the beginning of his healing process, but that was okay. He already felt so much better. It was thanks to Rocco, mostly, and he wanted Rocco to realize that. He wanted to give his mate the same — a shoulder to cry on, an ear that would listen to what he had to say. A heart that would forgive whatever there was to forgive — if there was anything at all. Someone who would be there for him — who would love him. It might be too soon to talk about love, but Cam wanted that. He wanted what Ox and Dasha had. He wanted something of his, something that had nothing to do with what had happened to him.

That would only happen if Rocco could give them a chance, though, and so far, he didn't look like he would.

"I thought you wanted to be with me," Cam said.

Rocco shook his head slowly. "Of course I want to be with you. That doesn't mean it's the best idea, though."

"Shouldn't we make that decision together?"

"Why? We can't be in a relationship if we don't both want it, and I don't."

"That's a lie." Cam was convinced of that. A few days ago, he might have let it go, but not now. No more. After everything Rocco had done for him, after the time they'd spent together in the infirmary, on the roof, and in his bedroom, he knew Rocco wanted him as much as he wanted Rocco. That didn't mean things would be easy for him alone, or that all their problems were solved, but it did mean that Cam knew

Rocco was lying, or rather, that even though he was convinced of what he was saying, it wasn't true. "You would never hurt me," he said.

Rocco put his plate down onto the tray, and Cam couldn't help but notice he'd barely eaten. "How can you know that?" Rocco asked. "We don't know each other."

"We do. You've been spending time with me for weeks."

"And you refused to talk to me for most of that time," Rocco pointed out.

"That doesn't mean I haven't been watching you. It doesn't mean I haven't gotten to know you. I have, and I know you would never hurt me. Whoever said you were dangerous was talking bullshit. I don't know if they were trying to keep you away from other people, to make you feel guilty, or whatever else, but it doesn't matter. It was a lie, and it still is. You would never hurt anyone. You don't have it in you. You wouldn't be a doctor otherwise, and even though I don't know Win well, I know he wouldn't allow you to stay here if that were the case. Whatever happened, Rocco, you need to forget and forgive yourself. You need to realize that you're a loving man, that you have a lot of friends, and that you truly would never hurt anyone." That was the only way they would be together. Cam didn't know how that would go, but he needed Rocco to see that it was a possibility.

He wanted it to be one.

Rocco opened his mouth, but before he could add anything, someone knocked on the open door. The sound was frantic, and both Rocco and Cam turned to look at whoever was there.

"Something happened," Tali said. He was paler than usual, and that made Cam realize that something was wrong. Rocco jumped from his chair, already moving toward Tali. "Who?" he asked.

Tali shook his head. "No one for now, but Tony hasn't

come back from his last mission," he said.

Cam didn't know Tony or most of the assassins. They were Rocco's friends, though. They were his *family*, and he was worried about them.

"Do we know anything?" Rocco asked.

"Not as far as I know. Win came over to tell me we should keep the infirmary ready, just in case. He's sending someone to look for him."

But in the meantime, they didn't know what had happened to Tony, or whether they would see him again. Cam didn't have to be told to know how bad that was.

Chapter Five

Tony still hadn't come home. Rocco wasn't sure what to do with that. He was worried, just like everyone else, and he hated that there was nothing he could do.

Win had sent out almost everyone to try to find Tony, but so far, they hadn't been able to locate him. Rocco knew that going out there himself wouldn't help, but he still had the instinct to do just that. He wasn't an assassin, though, not anymore. Besides, Cam needed him. Rocco had to stay with his mate to make sure nothing happened to him, although these days, it was starting to feel like an excuse.

Cam was doing well. Leaving the infirmary had truly done him good, and Rocco was starting to realize that it wouldn't take him long to heal. His body was still going slowly, but his mind was taking giant steps, mostly thanks to Gentry and, of course, Cam, who was working hard. He still had nightmares—and Rocco was more than aware of that since he slept beside him—but apart from that, Cam seemed to be doing extremely well.

Rocco wasn't.

It wasn't just Tony's disappearance, either. Having to sleep every night next to Cam was making him nervous. He knew Cam wasn't ready for anything, and he would never expect him to be. Besides, Rocco wasn't after something physical, although he couldn't deny that if he had a chance, he'd have sex with his mate. It was more than that, though. Having him so close, being in such an intimate position with him, made him want more.

He wanted Cam in his life to stay. He wanted them to bond. He didn't even care if they never had sex. He and Cam hadn't talked about what they liked, and Rocco wasn't about to ask, considering the situation. But it felt like they were half together but not quite, and it was driving Rocco crazy. He realized now wasn't the best moment to ask, though, which was why he'd kept his mouth shut so far.

For once, he was sitting at the kitchen table, eating breakfast. Cam was still sleeping, and Rocco hadn't wanted to stay in the room. He needed to move, and this was better than nothing. It also meant that when the door opened and Armand came in, Rocco was right there to hear the latest news. Win had sent Armand out to find Tony, and everyone had a lot of faith in him. He, more than anyone, could slither into people's lives and find out information.

Everyone in the kitchen turned, but Armand shook his head, his meaning clear.

Rocco's shoulders slumped. He'd been hoping, even though he knew he probably shouldn't have.

"What now?" Dasha asked from next to Rocco.

Rocco shrugged. "I have no idea. If Armand wasn't able to find Tony, I don't know who can."

Dasha slowly nodded. "There has to be something we can do."

"I wish I could say yes, but what? You couldn't shimmer to him, and that's the only way we had to find him."

They stared at each other, both wondering the same thing. They didn't get an answer, though. Rocco knew there wasn't one.

Even though Rocco had wanted to stay away from Cam and not wake him, he couldn't stay here anymore. He grabbed a plate for his mate, then headed out. If Cam was still sleeping, Rocco could leave the plate there and go to the infirmary. He could find something to do there.

Before he could climb the stairs, a commotion at the other set of stairs, the one that led to the garage, made him stop. He walked back into the kitchen to find that the stair door was open and people were rushing out. Since he had no idea what was happening, he put the plate back on the counter in the kitchen and followed everyone.

"What's going on?" he asked Ox, who was standing at the top of the stairs looking down.

Ox turned to look at him with wide eyes. "It's Tony," he said

Rocco frowned and pushed people aside so he could go downstairs. If Tony had been found, he needed to get to him. He needed to get him to the infirmary, and probably as soon as possible. He could imagine that the people who'd had Tony for almost a week hadn't been making sure he was fed and comfortable.

It *was* Tony. He was slumped in front of the warehouse by the door. Everyone was staring at him as if they didn't quite know what to do with him. Rocco got angry, even though he understood. They weren't doctors. They weren't nurses or Nix, so they didn't know what was happening or how to help.

He pushed Milo toward the house. "Get me the twins," he snapped before turning his attention to Tony.

Tony was awake. It was a small miracle considering all the wounds and the blood Rocco could see on him, but he was grateful. If Tony was conscious, he might be able to tell him what hurt and what had been done to him. That would help him help Tony.

Rocco crouched next to him and gently touched his cheek. Tony jerked as if he hadn't seen Rocco come closer, and maybe he hadn't. He might be conscious, but that didn't mean he was all here. "Tony?" Rocco asked. He didn't want to startle the man, but he needed to ask Tony questions if it was at all possible.

Tony blinked. "Rocco?"

"Yeah. It's me. You're home."

To Rocco's surprise, Tony's face scrunched, and tears escaped his eyes. Rocco had no idea what to do. He was used to dealing with pain and wounds and blood, not with tears. Still, since no one else came closer, he put a hand on Tony's shoulder and squeezed.

Tony winced. Rocco jerked his hand away, but he was relieved to see Tony was done crying already. "You're in pain," he said.

"That's not why I was crying. I'm so sorry. I told them about the warehouse. I told them where it is, even though I tried not to. They hurt me, but they had someone else, too, and when they started torturing him, I had to do something. I had to stop them."

Rocco leaned back. If what Tony was saying was true, someone, whoever it was, knew where the assassins lived. That meant that all of them were in danger, and his mind went straight to Cam, who was still sleeping in his bed upstairs.

Shit. "How much time do we have?"

Tony shook his head. "I don't know."

"What about the other person who was tortured? Do you know what happened to them?" Rocco wished the twins would arrive soon. Not only did they need to heal Tony, but apparently, they needed to evacuate the warehouse. Luckily, they had a plan in place for that, but it wasn't going to be easy anyway.

Tony shook his head again. "He shimmered me here then left. I don't know where he went."

"Okay. If he was able to shimmer around, then he must not be as badly wounded as you are." A movement caught Rocco's attention, and he turned to see the twins standing there, looking at him with wide eyes.

He gestured them closer. "Shimmer us to the infirmary. He needs to get there right away. Jolyn, tell Win that the warehouse needs to be evacuated. Someone found out about it."

Rocco took Tali's hand, and Tali crouched next to him, putting his other hand on Tony's thigh.

The next thing Rocco knew, they were in the infirmary. Tony was on the bed, curled onto himself, and he was crying again. Rocco wanted to reassure him, to tell him that everything would be okay, but he couldn't. He didn't know if everything would be okay. He could only pray it would be the case, but he didn't want to lie to anyone, least of all Tony, in this situation.

"What do you need me to do?" Tali asked.

"We need to check for broken bones and to clean the wounds we can see. Start stripping him."

Tali nodded and went to work while Rocco headed to the sink to wash his hands.

He prayed that Ox would take care of Cam. He knew he probably shouldn't worry about that, especially since Ox had been right there when Tony had been found, but thoughts of Cam were never far from Rocco's mind. He had to focus, though. He couldn't lose someone else. He couldn't allow Tony to die, not when there was something he could do to help him.

Cam had no idea what was happening, but if he got his hands on whoever was making so much noise, he would strangle them. They were making a ruckus, and they'd woken him from the first good night's sleep he'd had in what felt like forever.

He reached out to the side, wanting to touch Rocco, but only finding an empty bed. He sighed and opened his eyes. Of course Rocco was gone. Cam really shouldn't be as disappointed as he was, especially if it was like he suspected, and it was already late. He had slept well. And while he was grateful that he had, he still wished Rocco had been there when he woke up. He rolled to his side, then pushed himself up into a sitting position. It still hurt, but it was getting better, and he was grateful. Even though he was still in some pain, he felt like he was finally taking his life back, and that was all he'd ever wanted.

He was still weak, though, and he felt that as soon as he tried to get to his feet. He probably should stay in bed, but he needed to use the bathroom, and he didn't want Rocco to regret his decision not to stick another catheter in him after he'd shifted back to human form. Cam had insisted he could go to the bathroom on his own if he needed to, and he was going to do just that.

His legs trembled, and he had to hold himself up on the bed, then the dresser, then the bathroom door. He almost fell on his face trying to close it, then realized that the bedroom was empty, so he didn't have to. He had to sit on the toilet to do his business, but he still counted it as a win, especially when he was able to wash his hands without falling. Once he was at the bathroom door, he eyed the bed, wondering if he would manage to get back into it. Before he could, though, someone ran by in the hallway.

Cam had to know what was happening, especially with the voices growing louder, so instead of getting back into bed, he headed toward the door. His knees felt like they were about to buckle by the time he got there, and he held himself up on the frame. He leaned outside into the hallway and looked around.

"What's going on?" he asked when he saw the people running around the hallway. Most of the bedroom doors were open, and he could see people packing. He had no idea what was going on, but he did know it couldn't be good.

No one answered, but Cam was close enough to hear what they were saying. The words made his stomach turn to ice. "What did he say?" a woman asked. Cam couldn't see who she was since she was in one of the bedrooms, but they were close enough that he could hear her every word.

"That he broke down. That when they started torturing that other guy, he told them everything they wanted to know," another woman said.

"Can't say I blame him. I still hate that we have to leave. I hate not knowing what's going on."

"You and me both. But there's no other solution to this. Tony told the people that were torturing him where the warehouse is, and they're probably already coming for us. We need to get out of here."

Cam leaned heavier against the doorframe. Someone was coming for them? The warehouse was under attack?

Shit. There was nothing Cam could do. Hell, he probably wouldn't even be able to get downstairs without tumbling down the stairs. He would hurt himself even worse, and if Tony was home and had been tortured, Cam already knew where his mate was—in the infirmary, taking care of Tony and not thinking twice about his own safety.

That thought made Cam want to strangle him and smother him with kisses at the same time.

He needed to get to Rocco. It didn't matter how weak his legs were. He could do it, even though he felt a hint of desperation at the thought of walking down two flights of stairs. There were no other solutions.

He took a deep breath, leaned against the hallway wall, and headed to the stairs.

By the time he was on top of the first flight, he was panting. He felt like there wasn't enough oxygen in the world to fill his lungs, but that wasn't enough to make him stop. Nothing would.

By the time he was looking down at the second flight of stairs, though, he was starting to wonder if he really could do this. He wanted to. If the warehouse truly was about to be attacked, if Rocco was in danger, Cam wanted to be with him. There was nothing he could do to help Rocco, to protect him, but still. He would never forgive himself if he wasn't with his mate and something happened.

He just wasn't sure he could make it down the second flight of stairs. Maybe if he sat down and dragged his ass off every step?

"What are you doing here?" a voice asked from the kitchen door.

Cam jerked so hard that he almost fell down the stairs. Two hands shot out to grab him, and he gave Julian a grateful smile. "You startled me," he explained.

"I can see that. That doesn't answer my question, though. What are you doing here? Shouldn't you be in bed?"

"The warehouse is under attack," Cam pointed out.

Julian nodded curtly. The man was always smiling, so it was weird to see the frown on his face. "I know that. Everyone is packing. You should still be in your bedroom."

"I need to get to Rocco."

"He's in the infirmary. Tony came back."

"I know. And I know he won't be able to focus on me, but that doesn't matter. If we truly are under attack, I want to be with him."

Julian hesitated. Cam didn't know what was going on in his head, and he didn't care. He gently shook Julian's hold off, then turned to the stairs again.

"You're really going to climb down even if you end up falling, aren't you?" Julian asked.

"I will. I told you. I can't stay away."

Julian huffed. "God help me with stubborn men." He wiggled his fingers out at Cam. "Come on. I'll give you a ride."

Cam blinked at him. "What do you mean?"

"I mean that your mate would have my head if he found out that I allowed you to climb down the stairs. I'll carry you to the infirmary. "

"I don't need you to carry me."

Julian arched a brow. "It looks to me like you do."

He wasn't wrong. Even though Cam wanted to do this by himself, he knew he wouldn't be able to. Instead of insisting, he held his arms out. Julian rolled his eyes, but he managed to get Cam into his arms without too many problems.

It was odd. The only person who'd carried Cam recently was Rocco, and while Cam knew it was impossible, he also wished that Julian were his mate right now. Luckily for him, there was only one flight of stairs to go, and Julian climbed down in a hurry. He kept looking around as if he expected something to happen, but they got to the infirmary door without a problem. Julian pushed it open with his shoulder, then stepped in.

Cam sucked in a breath. Tony was spread out on one of the beds, bloody and grimacing. He was conscious, which Cam supposed was a good thing, but he was obviously in pain, and Rocco and the twins were moving around him, taking things from the tables in the room, working on him, talking to each other.

The entire warehouse vibrated from an explosion. Cam whimpered and pressed himself closer to Julian, who wrapped his arms tighter around him. He managed to stay on his feet, but his eyes were wide. Rocco swore and looked around, jerking when he saw Cam was there. "What are you doing here?" he asked.

Cam shook his head. "I needed to be with you."

"Do you know what's going on out there? Was that an explosion?"

Julian's voice was grim when he answered for Cam. "I'm

pretty sure that whoever tortured Tony just found us," he said.

"Fuck. I can't move him, not yet."

Julian looked around, then gently put Cam on one of the chairs. "Stay here," he ordered. He turned to Rocco. "You're sure you can't move him?"

"Of course I'm sure."

"All right. That means we need to stay here. With the number of assassins around, it probably won't take them long to get rid of whoever's attacking us." Julian turned toward the door, then moved closer to look out the small window.

Cam held his breath. He had no idea what was going to happen, but he was terrified. He couldn't even go to his mate to be reassured, and he didn't try. Rocco had more important things to focus on, and Cam could stand on his own two feet for a while.

He was with Rocco, which was what he'd wanted. He could sit tight until they had to leave

What the fuck was Cam doing here? Rocco didn't have the time to think about that right now, but he also couldn't ignore it. "What were you thinking?" he asked him as he tried to focus on Tony.

"What do you think I was thinking? I woke up alone, and no one came to tell me what was going on. I had to find out by listening in to a conversation in another bedroom."

Shit. Of course he'd had no idea what was going on. Rocco had no idea himself, but it looked like the house was under attack, and he didn't know what to do about it. "You should have stayed with the others," he said.

"And leave you alone? I don't think so."

"It would have been safer than being here with me right now. We can't move. That means you can't leave the infirmary. You think that's going to help?"

Cam crossed his arms over his chest. "I don't care what you think. I wasn't going to run away while my mate was here in the middle of things."

Any other day, Rocco would have been happy to hear Cam claim him as his mate. Right now, though, he was angry, worried, and on the edge of panic. He needed to focus on Tony, but Cam's presence made it hard, as did the noises coming from inside the warehouse.

It felt like the building vibrated every so often, and he was pretty sure someone was trying to blast their way inside. Luckily for the assassins and their mates, Win had expected something like this to happen eventually. He hadn't wanted to risk it, which meant that he'd put security procedures in place. They had a plan for evacuation, and Rocco had no doubt it was already happening, but that wasn't all. There was a state-of-the-art security system, and apparently, it was giving the attackers problems. It wouldn't last forever, though. That meant that Rocco needed to fix Tony up as much as he could so that the twins could shimmer them away.

So he focused on that. He gestured at the twins to heal the open wounds after he'd cleaned them, and they got to work. They knew what to do. There were used to this. Of course, they didn't usually do it while under attack, but Rocco was positive they could deal with pretty much everything.

Still, it would have been easier to do if he hadn't been so worried about what was going on outside.

He supposed he should feel lucky that Julian seemed to have decided he would be their protector and was staying by the door, ready to kick the ass of anyone who wanted to come in. It was better than nothing, and it did help Rocco calm down. Whatever happened next, there was nothing he could do to stop it. The only thing he could do was to focus on Tony and make sure he was okay so that he wouldn't be in danger of dying by the time they could leave.

"Do you see anything through the window?" Cam asked Julian.

Julian shook his head. "Nothing much. I can *hear* a lot of stuff, though. Pretty sure those were shots, and someone is yelling as if their head had just been torn off. Wait. They wouldn't be yelling if they didn't have their head anymore, right?"

Rocco shouldn't be as amused as he was with Julian's words. They meant the assassins were defending the warehouse. Even though Rocco hadn't talked to anyone, when Jolyn had gotten to the infirmary, he'd told him Win was already aware of what was going on, and he was dealing with it. He wanted Rocco to focus on Tony, and that was what Rocco would do. Still, as soon as Tony was able to be moved, they were out of here. Rocco wasn't an assassin anymore. He couldn't barge into the fight and take things into his own hands, no matter how much he wanted to. Besides, he needed to protect Cam. Cam wouldn't be any safer if Rocco left.

"I think someone's coming, guys," Julian said.

Dammit. That was the last thing they needed.

"Wait. I'm pretty sure he went to the office instead of coming here. We're okay for now, but you should hurry," he told Rocco.

Rocco resisted the urge to throw something at his head. "What do you think I've been doing?" he asked.

"I'm not sure, but it's not enough. They're going to realize we're in here soon, and then we'll be in trouble. I don't have any weapons with me. I didn't expect to be attacked."

"No one expected to be attacked," Rocco pointed out.

He gestured at Jolyn to heal the wound he'd been cleaning. He needed to do x-rays to see if Tony had broken bones, but he couldn't do that right now. He couldn't be sure they had time. He bit his lower lip and looked around. Tali was there, cleaning a scalpel, and Rocco grabbed him. "You need to heal his bones," he said.

Tali's eyes were wide. "Which ones?"

"I don't know. I'm pretty sure he has at least a few broken bones, but we can't x-ray him. Can you still heal him?" It was a shot in the dark, but they needed to do something. They needed Tony to survive if they decided it was time to move him.

Tali shook his head. "I don't know. I can try, though."

"You do that. I'll check his legs and make sure he can use them if he needs to." Because if there was one thing Rocco knew about the assassins—including Tony—was that they would try to fight even if they were wounded. That meant Tony would eventually try to get up from the bed.

Sure enough, Tony grabbed Rocco's hand and pulled him close. "What's going on?" he asked. His voice was full of pain, and Rocco wasn't about to tell him what was actually going on. The risk was that Tony would get up and try to throw himself into a fight and hurt himself even more than he already was in the process. "Everything is fine. We're stabilizing you so we can take you away."

"Don't lie to me. I'm not deaf, even though I'm wounded. I can hear something is happening, and it's not good."

Rocco sighed. "You're right. Something *is* happening, but we have it under control. The twins are healing you, and Julian is standing guard at the door. I don't need you to hurt yourself even more to protect us. Stay right where you are. Please."

Rocco was pretty sure Tony wanted to protest, so he was surprised when he nodded and let go of his wrist. He wasn't going to look a gift-horse in the mouth, though, so he went to work. He had to cut Tony's jeans, and he winced at the sight of the open wounds on most of his skin. Someone had used cigarettes to hurt him, and there were deep cuts on both his thighs. They were going to be hell to clean, but it needed to be done before one of the twins could get to it.

"He's out of the office," Julian called out. He was by the door, looking out the small window.

He had a perfect view of the door to the stairs and the office, so Rocco knew he was telling the truth. "Can you do anything?"

"I'm going to try, but it would be better if we could all get out of here."

Rocco shook his head. "I need another ten minutes."

"I don't think we have another ten minutes," Julian snapped. He looked around, but they didn't keep weapons here. It was an infirmary, so why should they? "I'll do everything I can, but I swear to God that if I die in the process, I'll come back and haunt you," he told Rocco.

"And I'll welcome you in my house if you decide to do that. I need ten minutes. Please."

Julian nodded. "I'll give them to you. You need to finish healing Tony so we can get out of here as soon as possible."

They both had their orders, so Rocco went to work.

Cam was terrified, and the fact that there was nothing he could do made it even worse. Maybe if he could help defend himself and Rocco, he would feel better about what was happening. As it was, though, he was useless. He had to watch as Rocco and the twins worked on Tony while Julian got ready to defend them from whoever was coming. There was nothing he could do, even if he shifted. He was still wounded, and his otter form was small. Besides, he was also in pain, and that would make it near impossible to do anything. Walking down the stairs had sapped his energy, and now he wished he hadn't. Maybe if he'd stayed upstairs, things would be different.

They wouldn't be. Even if Cam wasn't there, Rocco still would be. He would still be trying to heal Tony as fast as he could so Tony could be moved. He would still be in danger. Cam might not be able to fight, but there had to be something he could do. He didn't know what, but he was about to find out.

Julian grabbed a scalpel from a nearby table, then turned to face the door. "Here we go," he murmured. The door opened.

Cam wasn't even sure what happened next. One moment, Julian was standing there, and the other, he screamed and jumped whoever was coming in through the door. The man stumbled back, but he quickly recovered, even though Julian had managed to cut his cheek. He threw himself at Julian, and Cam had to watch them fight. There was still nothing he could do. He wanted to help Julian. He wanted to help Rocco. He wanted to help Tony.

But instead, he was immobilized, unable to do anything but stare.

At that moment, he hated himself, but even more, the scientists who had made him into this. He might not have been a fighter even when he'd been in the best shape, but he could have helped. He could have done *something*. As it was, he could only stare as Julian got his ass kicked. No matter how hard Julian was trying to defend them, there was only so much he could do, and he was already starting to wane. Julian's arm hung by his side, probably broken. The man he was fighting was also dripping blood from his face and his arms, but he looked satisfied, as if this was what he'd come for.

It probably was.

Julian didn't stop, though. Instead of staying down, the way Cam would have, instead of giving up, he got to his feet again and threw himself at the man. The man blinked as if surprised, but that only lasted for a moment. Even though

Julian managed to get a punch in, soon, he was on the floor again, holding his arms to his chest. There was blood dripping from his cheek and his mouth, and Cam was pretty sure he would have at least one black eye.

That was, if he survived. Right now, Cam wasn't sure any of them would.

"Leave them alone," Julian snapped as the man turned toward the bed on which Tony was being healed.

The man laughed, shook his head, and strode toward Tony.

Cam had to do something. He looked around, frantic, and noticed another scalpel. He grabbed it. He'd never done anything like this, but it was better than standing there and doing nothing. He focused on the man and threw the scalpel at him. If anything, it would probably distract him.

He was stunned when the scalpel buried itself into the man's back. The man jerked and made a startled sound. He stayed on his feet, but he had to stop and try to take out the scalpel sticking out of his body.

He reached around, but he couldn't touch the make-shift weapon. It was too far down his back.

Then he turned his attention to Cam.

Cam sucked in a breath. He'd known what he was doing and that he was putting himself in danger. He was relieved he'd done it, even if he got hurt. He was giving Rocco more time, and that was what Rocco needed. It didn't matter if he paid with his own life.

He would have regrets, like not telling Rocco that he wanted to be with him, that he wanted him as a mate, but right now, there was nothing he could do about that. He was doing what he could to keep his mate safe, and he was proud of that.

The man moved toward him. Cam swallowed, wondering if it was over for him. The man grinned, his teeth dark with blood, and reached for Cam. Before he could touch him, a scalpel appeared out of nowhere and buried itself right in the guy's neck. The guy blinked before falling to the floor, blood spurting from the wound. He didn't move again, and Cam sucked in a relieved breath.

Cam blinked and peered around. Julian was on the floor, his eyes wide as he looked from the dead man to Rocco, who was still working on Tony and not even looking their way. "Did you see that?" Julian asked.

Cam shook his head. "Did I see what? Did you throw that scalpel?"

"Of course not. I wouldn't have been able to kill that guy from here even if I didn't have one arm out of commission. It was your mate. He didn't even look at the guy. He just grabbed that scalpel from the tray and threw it. How the fuck did he manage to hit him in the neck?"

Cam didn't know how to answer that, and he didn't have to. At that moment, Rocco stepped away from Tony and moved toward Cam. "Are you okay?" he asked. He ran his hands down Cam's arms as if trying to see whether he was wounded.

Cam nodded. "I'm okay. Well, at least physically. I'm freaking out, but that's not surprising." He wanted to ask how Rocco had done it, but he knew now wasn't the moment.

Rocco nodded. "You need to stay here," he said. Then he turned toward the door. Cam hadn't heard it until now, but someone else was coming.

"Can Tony be moved?" Cam asked, the desperation evident in his voice.

Rocco shook his head without looking at him. "The twins are healing him, but we need to buy them time."

"We're going to get everyone killed."

Rocco finally flicked his gaze toward Cam. "We won't. You're going to stay where you are, and you won't move. I'll take care of everything."

Cam wanted to protest, but could he? There was nothing he could do. Arguing wouldn't help anyone, least of all Rocco, who needed to focus on what was happening. Cam needed to keep in mind that even though he'd only ever seen Rocco as his mate and a doctor, he'd been an assassin once. He had experience in this, even though he hadn't done it in a while. He could find whoever was about to come in and win.

Cam had to convince himself of that.

The door opened, but before anyone could attack them, Tali appeared next to Julian. He touched Julian's arm, shimmered next to Cam and Rocco, and Cam acted on instinct, grabbing the hand Rocco didn't have on Tony, then Tali's free one.

Together, they shimmered away. Cam just had the time to watch whoever was coming in a rush toward them, a gun held high so he could shoot them, but even though there was the sound of a shot, it didn't touch them. They were already gone by the time it made an impact with the chair Cam had been sitting in, and Cam's shoulders slumped in relief.

He had no idea where they were when they shimmered, but he didn't care. He let go of Tali's hand and wrapped his arms around Rocco, holding his mate close. He'd thought he would never have this. He'd thought that he and Rocco would never be able to be together, and they almost hadn't. Instead, they had a second chance, and he wouldn't waste it.

CHAPTER SIX

R occo had killed again. He'd known it would happen eventually, but he couldn't believe he'd done it in front of his mate. He'd put Cam in danger, but that wasn't the only disaster. He'd also revealed the monster he was, and he couldn't look at Cam. So he focused on Tony, even though it was hard.

He knew where Tali had shimmered them, of course. This had all been planned in case the assassins needed to flee the warehouse, and they were now in Gillham's infirmary.

It was as well-equipped as Rocco's infirmary, but it had the bonus of coming with a doctor. That meant Dallas was there to help Rocco as soon as he and the others arrived, and Rocco was grateful for that. Even though he was trying to focus on Tony, he couldn't stop thinking that he'd killed and that Cam had seen him do it. What would he think of Rocco now? Would he look at him in horror, or would he understand why Rocco had done it?

But that didn't matter, did it? Even though Rocco had done it for all the right reasons, he'd still killed. It wasn't the same as what had happened in the past, but it was still a death he knew he would never be able to forgive himself for.

"Rocco," Cam said.

Rocco shook his head. "Not now. You're okay. We're in Gillham. You should stick with Julian. I'll stay here and take care of Tony."

There was a pause before Cam snapped, "I won't allow you to ignore me, not in this kind of situation. Something happened, and I want to know what."

It was the last thing Rocco wanted to do. He didn't want to face Cam right now. He didn't want to see the fear in his mate's expression.

Because there was no way that Cam felt anything but fear for him. He was a killer.

Two hands landed on his shoulders, and he was turned around forcefully. He glared at Julian, who shrugged and tilted his chin at Cam. "He wants to talk to you, and as far as I'm concerned, he's the boss."

Rocco pointed at him. "I could kill you with barely a thought."

Instead of looking afraid, Julian grinned. "Don't think I didn't notice that. I have *so* many questions for you."

"What questions?"

"Like how you managed to get the scalpel into that guy's neck without even looking at him. That is *not* natural." Julian's eyes widened. "Wait. Is that your superpower? Do you have, like, infallible aim?"

That *was* Rocco's power, but instead of answering Julian, he looked at Cam.

His mate was sitting on a chair, but he was pale, and his hand trembled as he reached for Rocco. Rocco couldn't have stayed away even if he wanted to, and he didn't. He was afraid of finding out what Cam thought about him, but not so much that he would leave Cam behind when Cam obviously needed him.

Rocco moved closer. He allowed Cam to take his hand and tangle their fingers together, then he simply stood waiting. If Cam told him he never wanted to see him again, then that was what Rocco would do. He would stay away, no matter how much it hurt.

"Do you want to talk about what happened?" Cam asked instead.

Rocco shook his head. "There's nothing to talk about. I need to go to Tony."

"You don't. The other doctor is already taking care of him. Besides, you need some time. You're shaking."

"I'm fine. Fine enough to take care of Tony." Rocco almost smiled when Cam rolled his eyes. Cam wouldn't have done that even a few weeks ago, but now he was becoming surer of himself and confident. It was a lovely sight, and Rocco didn't know what would happen if he wasn't allowed to see it anymore. He supposed he was about to find out.

Cam let go of Rocco's hand and held his arms out. "Come on. Carry me out of here. I don't want to be in the doctor's and the Nix's way."

Rocco could only obey. If he was honest with himself, he wanted out of the infirmary, too. He didn't belong here, even though he was a doctor, and Cam was right. Tony was in the best of hands, and Rocco could focus on his mate, which was all he ever wanted.

So he gently took Cam in his arms, then carried him outside. When they stepped out of the infirmary, Cam's expression broke into a delighted smile, and he tilted his face up to meet the sun. "This place is incredible," he murmured. He looked at Rocco. "Can you tell me where we are?"

"Gillham Pack territory."

Cam slowly nodded. "I see. I should have guessed this is where we would end up." His expression softened, and he cupped Rocco's face. "What's going on? And don't tell me it's nothing, because I'm not an idiot and I'm not blind. Something is wrong with you, and I want to know what it is."

Rocco was tempted to repeat that he didn't want to talk about it. It would be his right, even though Cam was his mate. But he *never* wanted to talk about this, and he knew that time wouldn't change that. Cam also deserved an answer for what he'd seen, no matter how little Rocco wanted to give him one.

"I just killed a man in front of you. That's what happened."

Cam rolled his eyes again. It was something he was doing more often now, and even though Rocco knew it wasn't a good thing, he was delighted. "I saw you kill him. Again, I'm not blind. I'm just not sure why it hit you so hard. I mean, you were an assassin. You're used to killing people, aren't you? And that guy was going to hurt us. You couldn't have done otherwise."

Rationally, Rocco knew that. His mind wasn't always rational, though, not when it came to his past. "Are you okay?" he asked instead of answering Cam's question. "And don't roll your eyes at me. I truly just want to know how you are."

"I'm fine. Why don't you put me down on the bench and sit next to me?"

Once again, Rocco obeyed, at least in part. He settled Cam onto the bench, but instead of sitting next to him, he took a step back.

There was a flash of pain in Cam's expression, but he didn't say anything about it. "Now tell me what's really going on in that head of yours. And don't tell me you're like this because you killed someone. That can't be right."

Rocco raked a hand through his hair and started pacing. "Don't you see, though? It's what I do. I hurt people."

"That guy was going to hurt *me*. I'm not angry with you for killing him."

"Him, maybe not. He deserved to die, if anything because nothing else would have stopped him. But what about the other man I killed? The one who hadn't done anything to deserve it?"

Cam frowned. "I don't understand what you're talking about."

It was the last thing Rocco wanted to do, but he had to. He sucked in a breath, then explained. "It's the reason I retired. The reason I'm not an assassin anymore. I was on a job a long time ago. My last job. I killed my mark, but also a bystander. I still don't know what happened, even though I've thought about it for years. The guy wasn't supposed to be there, and I didn't know he was, but that doesn't change the fact that I killed him. It doesn't change the fact that I hurt someone who didn't deserve it, and I never took another job after that. It's why I became a doctor. I want to help people instead of hurting them."

Rocco couldn't read Cam's expression, and he hated it. He expected Cam to tell him he never wanted to see him again. He expected Cam to be disgusted by him and relieved that they'd never bonded.

Instead, Cam held his hand out again. "You made a mistake," he said softly.

Rocco took his hand because he couldn't afford not to, not if this was going to be the last time they had this kind of contact. "I made a mistake, yes. I took a man's life away. A man who hadn't done anything, who didn't deserve it.

"And you've been atoning since then. I can only imagine what you've been through and what you're still going through. But what happened wasn't your fault."

"I killed that man. I was the one who did it. No one else."

"Did you do it on purpose? Did you know he was there, that he was innocent? Did you kill him anyway?"

"Of course not. I told you I didn't know he was there. My mark was supposed to be alone."

"Then as sorry as I am for that man, it wasn't your fault, and what just happened wasn't, either. You were doing your job, and you've been hurting and regretting what you did ever since. And today? You saved my life and Tony's, and probably everyone else's in that infirmary. And damn, what an aim you have. I'm not as impressed as Julian, but I can't deny it *is* impressive."

Laughter bubbled in Rocco's chest, and he let it out. "Julian is right. That's my superpower, as he calls it. I have a precise aim, even when I'm not looking. Whatever I throw always hits its mark." That was what had made him such a good assassin, and what had destroyed him. He'd been aiming for his target, but the other man had stepped in between, and one knife had hit him instead while the other went on to the target and killed him.

Rocco was still not okay with what had happened, and he didn't think he ever would be. But maybe, just maybe, he could forgive himself. If Cam had, why shouldn't he?

Cam should have realized he wasn't the only one tortured by the past. He didn't know how he'd missed it, except that he'd been focused on himself and his healing. Still, it wasn't a good excuse. Rocco had needed him, and he hadn't been there.

But now, he was.

He didn't know what was going to happen between them, but he wasn't going anywhere. Almost losing Rocco, being afraid for both their lives, had made him realize even more than before that he wasn't living his life. It was too easy to imagine what he could have lost if he hadn't rushed to the infirmary and if Rocco hadn't managed to kill that guy. He never wanted to go through something like that again, and the best way to make sure it didn't happen was to stick with Rocco.

It wouldn't be a hardship. Cam couldn't deny, at least not to himself, that he'd been falling in love with his mate for a while. He hadn't allowed himself to admit it because he'd been afraid, and he still was. He wasn't going to let fear rule his life, though, not anymore. He'd done enough of that already. That choice was probably the most terrifying thing he'd done until now, but he'd made a decision, and he wouldn't back down. He wanted his life back. He wanted to be with Rocco, and he wanted to stay at the warehouse. Well, that was, if the warehouse was still the assassins' home after this. Cam doubted that would be the case, though. Someone knew who they were and where they lived, so they couldn't stay there. But wherever the assassins were going, he was going, too.

He didn't tell Rocco that. His mate needed a moment to digest what had just happened and to wrap his mind around the fact that even though he'd killed a man today, he'd done it to save Cam's life. That was nothing to be ashamed of. Cam didn't know how he would feel if he killed someone, but he would never have to, hopefully. Still, if someone was about to kill Rocco, he wouldn't hesitate one second. He probably would feel guilty afterward, too, but he would never doubt that it was the right thing to do.

"I should probably go back to Tony," Rocco murmured. His gaze had moved to the door.

It was Rocco's job, so Cam wouldn't stop him if he was needed, but he doubted that was the case. "It looked to me like the doctor had everything in hand," he pointed out.

Rocco smiled at him. "Probably. Dallas is better equipped than I am. He doesn't have to hide in the infirmary, and he worked in a hospital, so he has more experience than I do."

"You can go if you think it's the best thing to do. I won't stop you."

Rocco shook his head. "No. You're right. Dallas doesn't need me sticking my nose where it doesn't belong. I'll stay with you, unless you want some time alone. I realize that you've just been through a lot, and you probably need time to breathe."

Nothing could be further from the truth, so Cam shook his head. "I want you to stay with me. Please. I don't know this place, and I'm not exactly comfortable staying out here."

"I'm not going anywhere. Dallas can do this. Besides, Tali

and Jolyn are in there with him, as well as his own Nix assistant. He truly doesn't need me."

Cam was relieved. He might have decided not to let fear rule him anymore, but that was easier to think than to actually carry out. He suspected he would always be afraid. There was nothing he could do about that, except fighting the fear and living his life.

Footsteps made him turn toward the forest. It was beautiful and wide, but he could see a path leading to the infirmary, and he tensed. Logically, he knew they weren't in danger. Rocco had told him they were in Gillham Pack territory, which meant they were safe. Cam was still nervous, though, and when he reached for Rocco, he was relieved that his mate moved closer. Together, they waited until whoever it was appeared. Cam looked at Rocco as soon as the man did, and he was relieved to see his mate smile.

"Rocco," the man said. "I heard there was a bit of a mess at the warehouse?"

Rocco sighed. "They found us. I'm not sure what happened there yet. It was a bit of a mess, but we got Tony back. Pretty sure the warehouse is a loss, though."

The man patted Rocco's shoulder. "Don't worry about that. It's not your job. It's mine." The man turned his attention to Cam. "And who is this? One of your patients?"

To Cam's surprise, Rocco beamed. "This is Cambridge, but you can call him Cam. At least, that's what he told me when I tried to call him Cambridge."

Cam snorted. "That's because I'm not crazy about my name." He wasn't sure what his mother had been thinking, but he supposed she had a theme, considering his brother's name was Oxford. "And it's a pleasure to meet you," he told the man.

The man was smiling. "I'm Kameron."

Cam knew the name. "The Gillham pack alpha." And

council member.

Kameron nodded. "Got it in one. I'm happy to see you're both okay."

"For now," Rocco said. "But I'm pretty sure we're homeless."

"And I just told you to let *me* worry about that. You're welcome to stay with the pack for as long as you need."

"That's not going to be easy, considering we're supposed to be secret." Rocco hesitated. "Have you heard anything from the warehouse? Do you know what happened to the others?"

Kameron nodded. "Win called me. They have everything under control, but you're right. You can't stay there anymore."

Cam hated being right. Even though he'd only left the infirmary a few days ago, he still considered the warehouse his home. It was weird, because he hadn't realized it was becoming that, but he couldn't deny it, and now he was losing it. He could deal with it, though. He could deal with everything as long as his mate was with him. It was corny, but it was the truth.

"Did you bring anyone else with you?" Kameron asked.

"Tony and the twins. Julian, too. We were in the infirmary when we were attacked, and we couldn't stay there. I have no idea what was happening in the rest of the warehouse."

"You did good. And don't worry. This situation is why this plan was put into place. Dallas is working on Tony?"

"He is."

Kameron nodded. "I sent an enforcers' team to the warehouse, just in case. I also have someone already looking for another place for you guys to stay. It's probably going to take a bit to replace what the warehouse was, but in the meantime, we'll find everyone a place to stay. None of you will be abandoned. The council won't allow that. You work for us, and that means we'll take care of you."

Cam knew that even though he didn't work for the council, the same went for him. Rocco wouldn't allow him to be homeless, and besides, they were mates. Wherever Rocco went, Cam went, too, even though they weren't bonded yet.

"You should relax," Kameron told Rocco. "You're not an assassin anymore. You're a doctor. Focus on being safe, and on your personal life."

Cam flushed. Were they that obvious? They hadn't even done more than holding hands. "You know?" he asked

Kameron's smile was gentle. "Whatever the two of you are, it's none of my business. Rocco, I know you won't listen to me, but you shouldn't go back to the warehouse. I know they're your family and that you worry, but they're safe."

Cam shared Kameron's opinion that Rocco wouldn't listen. Hell, he didn't want to stay here, either. His brother was still at the warehouse, and he needed to see that Ox was okay with his own two eyes. Once he knew, he would be able to focus on Rocco and their future.

Because they had a future. He hadn't been sure until now, but after almost losing everything, he wasn't going to give Rocco up easily, and he also wouldn't allow Rocco to think of himself as a monster. He wasn't. He was Cam's, and even though it was probably selfish, that was all that mattered to Cam.

Rocco only stayed away from the warehouse until he was sure all of the attackers had been dealt with. No matter what Kameron said, he needed to go. The assassins were his family, and he couldn't abandon them in this time of need. So when Dasha appeared in front of the infirmary, he took the chance. "I need you to shimmer me back to the warehouse," he told Dasha.

Dasha startled, taking a step back. Maybe Rocco should have given him some time to get used to this new place. He'd been here before, but only sporadically. Rocco was the only one who was comfortable with the pack. The other assassins tended to stay away, even Dasha.

"Rocco," Dasha said. He moved closer again. "I'm so glad to see you're okay. I wasn't sure. No one is."

"What happened?"

"We kicked their asses. That's what happened." Dasha's expression became fierce. "There weren't a lot of them, but we made sure they knew they shouldn't attack us again. What about you?"

"The twins shimmered Tony and us here. Julian, too." Although Rocco had lost sight of him, he wasn't worried. Julian was his own man. He could do whatever he wanted. Still, he was grateful that Julian had brought Cam to him. Even though he hadn't been happy to see Cam in the beginning, he could imagine how hard it would have been for him to be here while he had no idea what had happened to Cam or where he was.

"Great. Now, I need you to shimmer me back. I want to make sure everyone is okay."

"Kameron told you to stay here," Cam said from his bench.

Rocco didn't glare, only because it was his mate talking, and he realized that Cam was probably afraid of being left here on his own. "He did, but even though he's my boss, he doesn't live my life. I can go wherever I want. Besides, you heard Dasha. The fighting is over. Now, I need to heal the wounded."

To Rocco's surprise, Cam nodded and rose on his feet. "You're right. They need you. I'm coming, though."

Rocco shook his head. "You're tired, and I don't know what the warehouse will be like. You should stay here. The twins are here, so you won't be entirely alone."

Cam didn't seem to have a problem glaring at his mate, since he did just that. "I'm not letting you out of my sight," he said. "I almost did, and I can only imagine what would have happened if I hadn't been in the infirmary when you were shimmered away. If you're going, I'm going, too."

Rocco might not want to glare at his mate, but he *could* glare at Dasha when the man chuckled. Dasha raised his hands. "I have no business in this. Do whatever you want. But if you want to go, we should probably head out now. I talked to almost everyone to make sure they didn't need immediate medical assistance, and while they didn't, there are a few broken limbs and cuts the twins should probably attend to."

Rocco nodded. "They're inside. I'll grab one of them, and we'll be back right away."

Rocco left Dasha and Cam outside and headed into the infirmary. He was grateful he would have the opportunity to check in on Tony, even though he knew Tony was in good hands. Dallas was a great doctor, and the Nix he worked with was just as good.

He wasn't surprised to see the twins and Julian sitting on one side of the room. They didn't have anything to do except watch Dallas and Sei take care of Tony, and they would probably be grateful for the opportunity to leave.

"I'm going back," he told them as he got closer. "Dasha is here, and Cam and I are going back to the warehouse. I need one of you to come with me to heal the broken bones and cuts and bruises we'll find there."

For whatever reason, Tali looked away. He was sitting with his brother between him and Julian, who was staring at Tali as if he'd seen a ghost. He didn't even acknowledge Rocco, but Rocco didn't care. He just needed one of the twins.

Jolyn rolled his eyes and rose to his feet. "I'm coming. Those two have something to talk about, so it'll give them time."

Tali's head snapped to them. "What? We have nothing to talk about. I can come, too."

Rocco had no idea what was going on, and he didn't want to find out. He shook his head. "I only need one of you. The other should stay here. I don't want Tony to be alone with people he doesn't know."

"But—"

"You heard him," Julian said. "He wants you to stay here. I want you to stay here, too."

Tali's cheeks reddened. "You don't decide what I do."

"You're right. I don't. I'm asking you to *please* stay."

Rocco didn't have the time to ask what the fuck was going on, but he made a mental note to check in on Tali once everything was over. He nodded and headed back to the door, relieved when Jolyn followed him. "What's going on between those two?" he asked.

Jolyn shook his head. "Don't ask me. I want nothing to do with that."

"But something *is* going on."

Jolyn grinned. "Oh, definitely."

Again, it wasn't Rocco's business, so he didn't push. Instead, he and Jolyn headed outside. Dasha and Cam were talking, but they looked up when they heard the door, and Cam smiled. "Dasha says I can come," he said before Rocco could say anything. "I agreed to sit in a corner and stay still, and he says it's not going to be a problem."

"As long as you actually do what you just said. I don't want to have to worry about you, too, not when I have to work on our friends."

Cam shook his head. "I promise I'm not going anywhere or doing anything. I just want to be with you. Besides, I'm worried about them, too. My brother is still there."

Shit. Rocco should have remembered that. Of course Cam wanted to find his brother. "Let's go." He held a hand out, and Dasha took it. Cam and Jolyn linked hands, too, and together, they shimmered away.

The warehouse was a mess. Rocco had expected that, but it was still much worse than he'd thought. Dasha and Jolyn had shimmered into the infirmary, where the wounded were being taken. Dasha was right—mostly, it looked like broken bones and cuts, so it shouldn't be too bad. Everyone Rocco could see was conscious, and when Ox saw his brother shimmer into the room, he cried out and rushed to them. Rocco was sure Ox would keep Cam out of trouble, so he focused on the wounded. All of them were talking, and he was so relieved that his knees almost buckled.

"I wasn't sure you were coming back," Win said.

"I wouldn't have left at all if I'd been alone."

"And Tony?"

"In good hands. Dallas and his people were taking care of him when I left, and Tali is with him."

"We're missing Julian." Win looked worried.

Rocco was happy to be able to relieve him. "He came with us. He was the one who brought Cam down to the infirmary."

Win sighed. "Thank God. He's not an assassin, but he's kind of become part of our family, and I was worried. You said Cam was with you, too?"

"He was. He's with his brother right now, but you can talk to him while I take care of everyone.

"I will. I'm curious to find out what happened here. We took the body out, so you don't have to worry about that."

Rocco wasn't sure he wanted Win to find out what he'd done. Win was one of the few who knew Rocco's history and the reason he'd retired. He'd never blamed Rocco, no matter how much Rocco had blamed himself.

But there was nothing Rocco could do if Cam, Julian, or one of the twins told Win what he'd done. He knew Win would understand, and that he wouldn't have anything to say about it. Cam's reaction was enough to prove that to Rocco. He was still worried, and he always felt like he should never have killed, but he knew in time, that reaction would pass. The only reason he'd killed that man was to protect his mate and his friends, and no matter how bad he felt about it, he would do it all over again if he had to. His mate was more important than his self-loathing.

The warehouse was a mess. It was as if a bomb had exploded. Cam winced. It hadn't been a bomb, but it might as well have been. Now the assassins didn't have a home, and it was going to be hard to find them a new place to stay, whatever Kameron had said.

While Rocco went to work on their friends, there was nothing Cam could do, so he listened in on the conversation Win was having on his phone. He was trying to find everyone a place to stay until they had a new warehouse, wherever that would be. Cam was relieved he wasn't in Win's place. It sounded like a nightmare, and even though he felt guilty about it, he was grateful he and Rocco had already been offered a place in Gillham. Still, he knew it had to be weird for the assassins to have to move, and even weirder to be without everyone else. They were family, and they were incredibly close. Cam had seen that when some of them had visited the infirmary, and he'd listened to the stories his brother had told him.

But whatever would happen, no matter how hard it would be, the assassins *were* a family. That meant they would get over this. That was a relief, and Cam relaxed, even though the room around him looked terrible.

"I was so fucking worried," Ox murmured. He hadn't left Cam's side since Cam had come back, and Cam didn't want him to.

He hadn't had much time to think about his brother while he and the others had been under attack, but he'd been worried. Hell, he'd been terrified. He'd just gotten his brother back. He didn't know what he would do if he lost him again. He had no intention of finding out, either.

"Do you think we'll end up in the same place?" he asked. When Ox arched a brow at him, he tilted his chin toward Win. "He's looking for a place for everyone. Do you think you'll be with me in Gillham, or will you have to go somewhere else?" Cam would understand if that happened, but he hoped it wouldn't. Even though he'd been keeping Ox at arm's length since he'd come back, now that he'd decided that needed to stop, he wanted to be able to do that. He wanted to become his brother's best friend again. He wanted them to be as close as they'd been before he'd been taken.

Ox scowled. "I don't care where Win says I have to go. I'm not leaving you behind. If you're in Gillham, then Dasha and I will be, too."

"As long as you're allowed."

"Win can't order me to do anything. It's different with Dasha, but I don't think we'll have to fight over it. Win is a good person. He'll understand I want to stay with you."

Cam bit his lower lip and looked around once again. "Have you ever used that building we inherited?" he asked.

Ox blinked. "I'm sorry?"

"You know. The building that Dad left us, the one where he used to work. It's kind of a warehouse, too, isn't it?"

Ox's eyes widened. "It is. I can't believe I forgot about that."

Cam wasn't surprised. So much had happened to both of them in the past few months, he'd barely remembered it. But looking at the damage all around him, knowing that the council and the assassins needed a new warehouse to keep everyone together, had made him remember. "If you haven't done anything with it while I was gone . . ."

"I haven't. What would I do with it? I'm not going to get any work done in there, that's for sure."

"Then do you think it could be a nice home for us? I mean, all of us?" Cam said, gesturing at the infirmary.

Ox smiled. "I hadn't thought about it, but now that you mention it, it makes sense. We have an empty building and a family to house. We should put them together."

It did make sense. Now that they'd thought about it, Cam almost started bouncing in his seat. Instead, he looked as Ox waved at Win.

Win came as soon as he was done with his phone call, arching a brow at the brothers. "You wanted me?

Ox and Cam looked at each other, then Cam asked. "Have you found anywhere to house the assassins?"

Win sighed. "Temporarily, yes. I found a spot for those who need one, and the others are going to find a place of their own. Don't worry. Both of you can go to Gillham. I already talked to Kameron, and he's okay with it."

Cam wasn't surprised. "What happens next, then? Does the council have another building to offer to the assassins so we can live altogether?"

Win shook his head. "Not so far. It's not like the council keeps empty warehouses around. They'll have to find and buy one, but that shouldn't be a problem. It's going to be a while before it can be fixed for all of us, though. In the meantime, we'll have to make do."

Cam and Ox looked at each other again. "About that."

Win blinked. "Yes?"

Cam swallowed. He wasn't sure why he was nervous, but he was. "Ox and I inherited a building from our parents. Our father, actually. He did his business there, but the warehouse has been empty for a while. We're not using it, and we're not planning on ever using it, to be honest." Cam had no idea what he would do with his life once he was healed, but whatever it was, he knew it wouldn't be away from Ox and Rocco. He would find something. He knew he would. He wouldn't need a warehouse for it, though.

Win slowly nodded. "Are you two offering me a warehouse?"

Cam laughed. He felt better now that he knew everyone was safe, unburdened in a way he hadn't been in a long time. "I guess we are? I mean, we don't need it. That, and the assassins are our family. I don't see why the council should have to buy another building when we have one we can use."

Win hummed as he thought. Cam knew there was a lot to consider, including how long it would take to transform an empty warehouse into a comfortable home for all of them. He didn't relish being displaced in the meantime, but he supposed the assassins would look at it like a vacation. Of course, they might still be required to work, but that probably wouldn't be a problem."

"Let me talk to Kameron," Win finally said. "And of course, it will depend on the state of the warehouse. But I'll be happy to accept unless Kameron and the council have something to say about it. Thank you. I have to say I didn't expect this, and it'll probably make my life easier."

"We can only offer the warehouse," Ox's said. He grimaced. "It's empty, and it's just what you would think of when you think about a warehouse. It's nothing like this place."

"That won't be a problem. The money the council would have invested in buying the place can be invested in transforming it into a home for all of us. You don't have to worry about that. I'll contact you as soon as I've heard from the council, but as far as I'm concerned, I do agree that this is the best thing we can do. Thank you, both of you."

"You don't have to thank us," Cam said.

The assassins were family. A weird family, a family Cam didn't know yet, but he would make sure that changed. He wasn't going anywhere, not when both his mate and his brother were here. It didn't matter where he lived, where he laid his head at night. He would be where his family was, and if that family had grown exponentially since his brother had found him? All the better.

CHAPTER SEVEN

Until now, Rocco had never understood why people took vacations. He'd hated the thought of being away from his things and his family for so long, and yes, a week or two felt like a long time. But now, the assassins had been disbanded until their new home was ready, and he, Cam, Ox, and Dasha, were on vacation.

He rolled his eyes at himself. He might not have known that vacations could be this pleasurable, but now that he did, he was going to spoil his mate and take him as often as he could.

They were lying in the sun with their feet dug in the grass. They'd hesitated between going to the beach or to somewhere in the country where they could be mostly alone, and they'd decided for the second one. They needed peace after what had happened, and Rocco was more than happy not to have to deal with crowds. Instead, they'd rented a chalet in the mountains, and in the middle of the summer, it was warm enough that they could bask in the sun without feeling cold.

And it was *silent*. Rocco wasn't used to this kind of silence. In the warehouse, everyone lived together. Even when some were asleep and others were out for business, it was still crowded. The chalet was anything but crowded, though, even with Ox and Dasha there. It was peaceful, the kind of peace Rocco hadn't known he could have. He knew he should take advantage of it. Eventually, he would have to go back to having a lot of people around, but that didn't matter, not as long as Cam was with him.

And he was. They hadn't talked about it, but Cam had made it clear he wasn't leaving Rocco alone, wherever Rocco went. That was more than okay with Rocco. He didn't want to leave Cam behind, either. He was more than happy to live with him and share a home.

"You're thinking awfully hard for someone who's on vacation," Cam pointed out from beside Rocco.

Rocco opened his eyes and smiled at his mate. It was incredible how quickly Cam was healing now. Rocco wasn't sure what it was, but it was probably just the normal way of things. Cam's body was almost back to the way it should be, although he would always have the scars. He still had nightmares, and those wouldn't be dealt with as easily as the physical wounds, but he was working on it. Rocco was, too.

It had taken having Cam in his life for him to realize that he was traumatized over what he'd done. He still felt guilty, and he doubted that would change anytime soon. But he was finally giving himself permission to live, which was a change for him. Until now, he'd kept himself isolated. He considered the assassins his family, but he'd still kept them at arm's length. He hadn't wanted to hurt them. He'd been convinced that the only thing he could do was hurt people, which was why he'd become a doctor. He'd wanted to make sure that he could help the people he hurt, heal them instead of wounding them.

But even though a man had once died because of him, it had been an accident. Cam was right. Even though the guilt was still there, Rocco needed to forgive himself. He wasn't sure he would ever be able to, but he was going to try. He owed his mate that, at the very least. "Just thinking," he said, smiling.

Cam smiled back. "Yeah? I was doing some thinking, too."

He looked nervous, and that made Rocco straighten in his chair. "Cam?"

Cam huffed. "How is it that you can always read me when I'm nervous?"

Rocco laughed. "I don't know. I guess we spend so much time together that I know what you're thinking."

Cam arched a brow. He looked better, with a hint of tan on his skin and freckles that had sprouted out of nowhere on his nose and cheeks. He was gorgeous, and he was Rocco's. "What am I thinking, then?" he asked.

Rocco shook his head. "I don't know what you're thinking *exactly*, but you're nervous. Does it have anything to do with me?"

"These days, everything seems to have to do with you. So yes." Cam hesitated, then looked at the house behind them. "Are Dasha and Ox inside?"

"I don't think so. Dasha told me they were heading out this morning, and not to wait for them for lunch or dinner. It looked like they had a date planned."

Cam sighed in relief. "Good."

It made Rocco blink at him. "Good?" The brothers were closer than ever, and it was nice to see.

Cam rolled his eyes. "I only meant that I don't want them in the house for what I'm about to suggest."

"And *what* are you about to suggest?"

Cam playfully glared at Rocco. "If you give me time to explain, I will."

Rocco mimed locking his mouth and throwing away the key, smiling when Cam laughed.

"All right. I'm talking." Cam sucked in a breath. "I've been thinking."

Rocco was tempted to joke around and tease him about it, but he didn't. He managed to keep his mouth shut just like Cam had demanded.

"I know we've never talked about bonding," Cam continued. "There hasn't been time. I was badly wounded, still healing, then we were attacked. So I realize we never talked about this. But I think we should now."

Rocco couldn't deny he'd thought about it, too, but he was surprised that this was where Cam's thoughts had gone.

They were together as a couple now. They hadn't talked about it, because it didn't need to be talked about, but after the attack, they were even closer. They hadn't had sex yet, but they'd kissed several times, and Rocco was more than fine with doing just that for the rest of his life if that was what Cam was comfortable with. He didn't need more. He just needed Cam in his life. "Are you saying you want to bond with me?" he asked, his voice a croak.

Cam nodded. "I think it's time. I love you, Rocco. I know I've never told you that, either, but it's the truth. I think I've loved you for a while, but I never allowed myself to admit it, and I didn't think I could be happy. I was terrified that you were going to break the trust I had in you, and I couldn't allow that to happen. But now I know you won't. I know you won't hurt me. I also know I'm not exactly the best mate I could be, though."

"That's not true."

"I have nightmares. I know I wake you up every night."

Rocco reached for Cam. He took his mate's hand, then gently pulled until Cam rose from his chair and came closer. Then, Rocco pulled him into his lap and wrapped his arms around him.

It was still strange to be physical with his mate. Rocco had worked so hard to stay away from Cam while Cam had been afraid of him and everyone else that even now, he always hesitated before reaching for him. But Cam was right. He'd been working very hard on himself, and he wasn't afraid anymore. "I don't care that you have nightmares," Rocco said. "I expected you to have them. You went to hell and back. I never told you what was done to me in that lab, but I still remember the aftermath. It took me months to trust people, and that includes Win."

"I just wish I had more to offer."

Rocco rubbed Cam's back. "And you will. If that's what you want, we can work up to it. I don't expect you to be perfect, Cam. I just expect you to be *you*."

Cam grinned. "Well, I *am* me, and I want to bond with you. I also want to have sex with you, since you're asking."

Rocco sputtered. "You do?"

Cam's smile softened. "I do. I allowed the scientists to take so much from me. I stopped living, even though I was free. I want that to change. I want to be myself again, and I want to be with you. I'm happy with the way our relationship has gone, but I want more. I think I *need* more. I need to show myself that I can be happy and that I can be with you."

"As long as you're sure."

"I am, and you should stop asking me before I change my mind."

At least now the fact that he wanted Ox and Dasha out of the house made sense.

Rocco allowed Cam to get up from his lap and take his hand to pull him to the house. He hadn't expected the day to go this way, but he wasn't surprised to see that once they were in the bedroom they shared, Cam took a small bottle of lube out of his bag. He blushed, then looked away. "I asked Ox to get it for me," he explained.

Rocco shook his head. "You thought of everything."

"Of course I did. I've been thinking about it for a while." He hesitated. "I don't know what I'm ready for. I don't know what I can give you right now."

"Whatever you're comfortable with."

That was what they did. Cam was still in some amount of pain, especially when he moved in certain ways, but Rocco knew that. He wasn't merely Cam's mate. He was also his doctor, and he knew where not to touch and where to touch. He made sure his mate was taken care of, sucking on Cam's cock until Cam was about to come. He loved having Cam wriggling under him, begging for more, digging his fingers in his hair to pull him closer. He never wanted this to end, and now, it wouldn't have to. He and Cam were in this forever.

Rocco had never thought he would have it. He'd thought he'd have to be alone for the rest of his life to keep everyone safe. It turned out that he wouldn't have to. He had Cam, and Cam wasn't going anywhere.

Once he was sure that Cam was in no amount of pain and about to come, Rocco moved upward. He pressed their naked bodies together, smiling when Cam whimpered and wrapped himself around him. Cam hooked his legs around Rocco's waist as if trying to pull him even closer. They couldn't get any closer than this, though. Cam wasn't ready for anything more, and that was okay. Rocco truly only wanted what Cam could give him.

So he kissed his mate as he thrust against him. Cam shuddered and cried out, and Rocco knew the moment had come. "You still want to bond?" he asked, his voice rough.

Cam opened his eyes. "More than ever. Bite me, Rocco."

Rocco obeyed. He would always obey his mate.

He pressed his mouth to Cam's neck, then slid his fangs into the skin there. Cam came almost instantly, and it made Rocco smile against his flesh. Yes, he might not have been with anyone for years before meeting him, but he still knew what he was doing, and he was more than happy to do it to his mate.

Then he stopped thinking, because Cam bit him, too.

He understood why Cam had come right away. He could feel Cam's pleasure coursing through the bond once it slid into place, and it was easy to follow that pleasure, to give himself up to it. It was easy to do just as Cam had done, to wrap himself around his mate, to hold him close.

Then they were one, their minds linked for the rest of their lives.

They flopped onto the mattress, sated in a way Rocco could never remember being.

"Damn," Cam murmured. "Why did we wait so long to do this?" He chuckled. "Wait. I know. It's because I wouldn't have been able to do this if I were still wounded."

It was that, of course, but it was also much more. Rocco never wanted to push Cam into something he didn't want. He'd wanted his mate to take this step, and he was grateful they had waited.

He wrapped his arms around Cam and pulled him closer, kissing his sweaty forehead. "How are you feeling?"

"Great. It's been a while since I felt this way." Cam hesitated. "Thank you."

"What are you thanking me for?"

"For not giving up on me. It would have been easy to do just that, especially when I kept pushing you away. But you didn't. You stayed by my side, and you made sure I knew how much you cared about me. So thank you. You're the only reason we have this right now. If it had been up to me, I probably would have run away a long time ago."

"Don't worry. I'm not going anywhere. If you need me to remind you of what we have every day for the rest of my life, that's exactly what I will do."

And it wouldn't be a hardship. Rocco wasn't going anywhere, and if Cam tried to run away, he'd remind him of what they had.

YOU MAY ALSO ENJOY THE FOLLOWING FROM EXTASY BOOKS INC:

False Friends
Catherine Lievens

Excerpt

The door slammed, jerking Dorran out of sleep. He opened his eyes, already scowling even though it was so early in the morning. He could tell by the light coming in through the window.

"Sorry," Eli said.

Dorran grumbled. "Not a problem."

"Try to get back to sleep."

Dorran softly snorted and buried his face against his pillow. That was easier said than done. Eli was used to getting up early to go to work. Hell, he was used to getting up in the middle of the night when he had a new case. Dorran, on the other hand, wasn't. That was one of the perks of working from home and making his own hours. He could get up when he wanted, which was what he did—or what he used to do anyway. Now, he and Eli had moved in together, and they were still trying to find a way to mesh their lives.

There was a rustling on the sheets, and Dorran opened one eye to see Princess Butterfly looking at him. He grinned and hooked an arm around the cat, dragging her closer. She purred and settled against his chest, and together, they drifted back to sleep. Dorran knew he wouldn't be able to fall deeply asleep again, though. He never could, not once he had woken up, especially when he'd woken up because of a slamming door.

Dorran rubbed his fingertips onto the cat's head. She was Eli's cat, but she loved Dorran just as much, which was a relief. Dorran had never had a pet, and he hadn't been sure what to do with her in the beginning. Now, she was already at home in his apartment, much more than Eli.

Dorran listened to Eli move in the bathroom. He smiled because even though he and Eli were still trying to find their way around each other and to settle in to living together without killing each other, he was happy. It was all he'd ever wanted since the two of them were teenagers. He'd broken up with Eli when they were kids, but he'd regretted it, even though he'd known he'd done the right thing. Things were different now, and he couldn't have been happier.

He and Eli had moved in together, and Eli's family was finally accepting Dorran. He hadn't thought it would happen, but even Eli's mother seemed to be happy with Dorran's presence in her son's life. He doubted she would throw them a wedding party or anything like that, but as it was, things were doing well.

Dorran was surprised when the next time he opened his eyes, he could tell several hours had passed. He listened, but the apartment was quiet, a sure sign that Eli was at work. The cat wasn't there, either. She was probably in the kitchen or the living room, staring out the window at the people who passed them on the street or sunning herself. Dorran had been abandoned, but he didn't blame her for it.

He stretched, pushing away the blankets. He had no idea what time it was, but from the sun streaming in through the window, it was about time to get up and start working.

He was looking forward to it. His life in the past several

weeks had been a mess. There had been the move, but before that, the reunion with his father, finding out he had a kid sister, and his father being accused of murder. Angus had been innocent, but it had taken a while for things to settle down. Some days, it felt like they still weren't, but Dorran could deal with it. He'd dealt with a lot worse.

He got to his feet, stretched again, and headed to the bathroom, only to freeze when he stepped inside.

The room was a mess. Eli's pajama pants were on the floor, surrounded by wet towels. Water had sprayed out of the shower to the floor, and Dorran almost slipped in it. The only reason he didn't fall on his face was that he managed to grab the doorframe. The toothpaste was open on the sink, a white blob on the ceramic. Eli's electric toothbrush was there, too, abandoned next to the faucet instead of on its base.

Dorran gritted his teeth. This was one of the things he wasn't yet used to. He wasn't a neat freak, but Eli was a slob, and there was no denying that. It was one of the reasons they were still trying to find a way around each other. Even though Dorran didn't demand everything be perfect in the apartment, he also didn't want their home to look as if pigs lived with them. He understood Eli was in a rush when he left home in the morning, but that didn't mean he couldn't put the cap back on the toothpaste tube.

He huffed, then carefully stepped into the room, avoiding the puddles.

It took him about ten minutes to clean up. He hung the wet towels, put the pajama pants into the laundry basket, and dried the puddles. He also scrubbed the sink since it was dirty with toothpaste. The entire time, he was scowling.

He relaxed once he was done and going through his morning routine. Eli was always in a rush in the morning, usually because he enjoyed staying in bed for far too long and snoozed his alarm at least twice. He cleaned when he came home, but Dorran worked in the apartment, and the bathroom couldn't be in this state. He couldn't jump around water puddles to get to the toilet for the entire day.

Once he was done, he grabbed his phone from the nightstand. He texted Eli, pointing out that he had cleaned the bathroom. Then, he headed to the kitchen, smiling when he found there was a pot of coffee already made. It was still warm, and he took one of the mugs in the cupboard as his phone vibrated.

I'll clean up when I come home, Eli had written.

Dorran scowled at the words. I know you will. But I still have to go to the bathroom for the entire day, and I'd rather not slip in one of the puddles and break my nose.

The tree dots waved on the screen. Sorry. I'll do better next time. Eli had added a winking emoji, and Dorran found himself smiling.

He'd been angry, and he still was, in a way. He realized that both he and Eli were having a hard time, though. They were used to living alone. Dorran had been on his own since he'd left his mother's apartment to go to college, and it wouldn't be easy for him to get used to having someone else around — someone who did things in a different way and who wasn't as neat as he was. He supposed he would get used to it, though. People usually did. There were millions of couples in the world, and most of them lived happily ever after once they moved in together. Surely, he and Eli could have the same thing.

Dorran realized he would have to compromise, but he knew he could do it. He was happy with Eli, and he didn't want to lose that or to fight. Still, he couldn't be the only one who made an effort, and he would make sure that Eli knew that.

You think you're cute, he wrote.

I know I am. That's why you love me.

Dorran rolled his eyes. I certainly don't love you because you leave a mess in the bathroom in the morning.

I already told you would clean up. I'm sorry, but I was in a rush.

I understand that. I might work from home, but it doesn't mean I don't understand the needs of a full-time job, especially a job such as yours. Dorran paused, trying to find his words. He didn't want to make Eli angry, not when his own anger was already fading. But we live together now. We have to think of the other. Leaving everything as it is wasn't a problem when you lived on your own, but I have to use the bathroom for the entire day.

You're right. Again, I apologize. I'll see you when I come home, okay? I have to go.

Dorran eyed the text. Was Eli angry? He couldn't tell from the words on the screen. Stay safe, he answered.

Always. Love you.

Dorran smiled. Eli wasn't angry. They would work this out, like they always did. They might fight and grumble, but they loved each other, and that was what mattered.

About the Author

Catherine is the creator of several series, most of them paranormal, including the Whitedell Pride Series and the Gillham Pack Series. While she graduated in translation, she decided to go the writer's way because it was more fun to create her own stories and characters.

She's been living in Italy for more than twenty years, but she's a daughter of the North—Belgium to be precise—and she misses it so much that she's already planning to move back.

She loves pizza—probably too much—her son, her pets, and of course, books. She sneaks some reading time into her schedule every time she has five minutes free from writing, demands from her various pets and son, and lastly, housework.

Connect with her:

lievens.catherine@gmail.com

BookBub: https://www.bookbub.com/authors/catherine-lievens

Website: https://authorcatherinelievens.wordpress.com/

Facebook: https://www.facebook.com/catherine.lievens.9

Facebook Group: https://www.facebook.com/groups/411788002341528/

Twitter: https://twitter.com/authorCLievens

Newsletter: http://eepurl.com/c-uvKn

www.ingramcontent.com/pod-product-compliance
Lightning Source LLC
Chambersburg PA
CBHW060635130626
46555CB00002B/813